Gill Sanderson, aka Roger Sanderson, started writing as a husband-and-wife team. At first Gill created the storyline, characters and background, asking Roger to help with the actual writing. But her job became more and more time-consuming and he took over all of the work. He loves it!

Roger has written many Medical Romance™ books for Harlequin Mills & Boon®. Ideas come from three of his children—Helen is a midwife, Adam a health visitor, Mark a consultant oncologist. Weekdays are for work; weekends find Roger walking in the Lake District or Wales.

Recent titles by the same author:

MALE MIDWIFE
A FULL RECOVERY
THE NURSE'S DILEMMA

MARRIAGE AND MATERNITY

BY
GILL SANDERSON

MILLS & BOON®

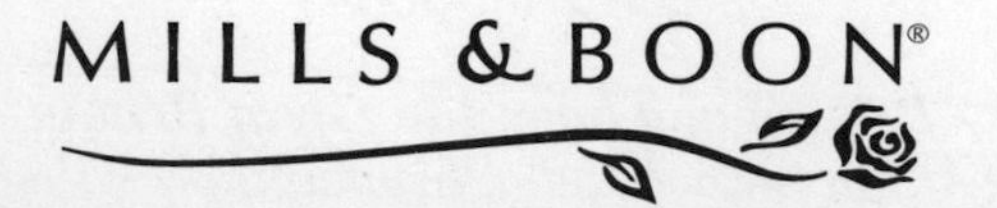

For Kate Conlan, Marie Murray and Sheila Walsh—
three writers of Southport Writers' Circle
who have helped me so much.

All the characters in this book have no existence outside the imagination of the author, and have no relation whatsoever to anyone bearing the same name or names. They are not even distantly inspired by any individual known or unknown to the author, and all the incidents are pure invention.

First published in Great Britain 2002
Large Print edition 2002
Harlequin Mills & Boon Limited,
Eton House, 18-24 Paradise Road,
Richmond, Surrey TW9 1SR

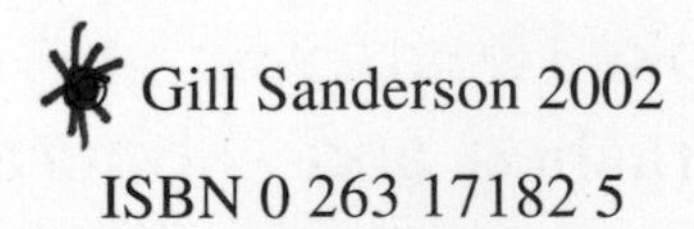

ISBN 0 263 17182 5

Set in Times Roman 16½ on 18 pt.
17-0702-50697

Printed and bound in Great Britain
by Antony Rowe Ltd, Chippenham, Wiltshire

CHAPTER ONE

THE night shift hadn't started well for Sister Angel Thwaite.

There were five babies in the neonatal unit, enough to keep her reasonably busy. Then came a desperate phone message. 'Come along to Theatre, meet your consultant there. We've got an urgent Caesarean section. Baby an estimated thirty-four weeks.' Angel winced. This was going to be hard.

The full horror of the situation only revealed itself as she talked to Linda Patterson, the paediatric consultant.

'We've no idea who the mother is. She was in a car crash, brought into A and E. Someone noticed the contractions, put her on a monitor. Her waters broke, heart rate and oxygen saturation levels crashed and she turned blue. We think she might have had an amniotic embolism.'

Angel nodded. Amniotic embolisms were very rare, but when they happened they were nearly always fatal. Amniotic fluid was forced into the mother's bloodstream. The mother died shortly afterwards, and usually the baby died, too. 'How's the baby?'

'Well, she's still alive.'

They were in a recess to the side of the main operating theatre. Angel had checked the Resuscitaire, the machine they would use to do what they could for the baby once it was born. Until then all they could do was wait and watch the team round the main operating table.

There was something about the green-clad team's demeanour that told her that the news wasn't good.

Suddenly they were in business. A bloody, sticky child was brought over to them.

'Mother didn't make it,' a voice said. All attention was now on the baby. It might make it—if they were lucky.

The baby was almost motionless. Angel did an instant Apgar test, assessing colour, heart rate, muscle tone, breathing and stimulus response. The baby scored four out of ten, not good. She was floppy, blue, there was little respiratory effort. She had suffered severe birth asphyxia. Her dying mother had not been able to give her the oxygen she needed.

Quickly she was sucked out then intubated and ventilated, oxygen being pumped into her system. After a while there seemed to be a positive response. She was less blue.

'Let's get her back to the unit,' Linda said.

Once in the unit the baby was quickly weighed—all decisions about feeding, drugs and oxygen depended on her weight. Then she was put in an incubator, ventilated again and connected to the full monitoring system.

Angel didn't exactly enjoy the work. This little girl was fighting for her life, you couldn't enjoy that. But technology and scientific knowledge were helping the fight, and Angel felt proud that she was helping, too.

Now heartbeat, blood pressure, temperature, respiration levels and oxygen saturation were all being monitored. Linda slid in an UAC line—an umbilical access catheter—through the umbilicus and then the baby was X-rayed to ensure that the tube to her lungs and the line were in place. She was written up for antibiotics and morphine.

'We really ought to have a signature for permission to give vitamin K,' Linda said. 'I need a parent.'

'The mother's dead and no one knows who or where the father is.'

So Linda gave the vitamin anyway. She couldn't let her charge have a smaller chance because of an administrative problem.

The little girl stabilised. 'I think she's going to make it,' Linda said. 'I didn't have high hopes but now she's got a fighting chance. I know you'll do one-hour observations and with any luck all should be well. I'm going off to bed. You know when and if to ring me?'

'I know, Linda. I don't think it will be necessary.' The nurse and the paediatric consultant beamed at each other. It might be late at night but they were happy with what they had done. A good evening's work.

Three hours later Angel was hard at work. There was no end to the paperwork. But no sooner had she started than there was a tap on her door and June Wright, her assistant nurse, peered round. 'There's a man come to see that new baby—you know, the one whose mother was killed. He says he's a doctor but not for this section.'

The door to the neonatal unit was, of course, locked. No one was allowed in unless they had the code to the door or a good reason for visiting.

'It's four o'clock in the morning. That baby has seen all the doctors she needs to see. Tell this one to come back later in the day.'

June disappeared, and then reappeared two minutes later. 'That man's getting very angry, Angel. He says the dead woman was his sister, he's her only relation. He's just joined the hospital—he's the new surgeon in the cardiac unit. If we want to check on him that's fine, but do it quickly. His name's Michael Gilmour.'

'What was that name?'

June looked surprised at Angel's horrified tone. 'He says he's Michael Gilmour. Angel, are you all right? You've gone very pale.'

Angel gripped the edge of her desk, looking downwards so that the junior nurse could not see the riot of emotions that must be so clear on her face. 'I'm a bit tired,' she gasped after a while. 'Working nights is never much fun, is it?' This was an excuse. So far she had been fine. 'Let's go and sec this man, shall we?'

She forced herself to stand and smile at June. Michael Gilmour wasn't such an uncommon name. How she hoped this man would be a stranger!

Rapidly she walked down the corridor, June having difficulty in keeping up with her. This was a nightmare, she needed to wake from it. If she could. At the ward entrance she peered into the little CCTV screen. The man was there, smiling unpleasantly up at the camera. He knew he was being watched. And Angel's nightmare was going to continue.

'Wait till I get to my room,' she told June, 'then let him in. Show him the baby, tell him anything he needs to know. Tell him he can't see me—that is, he can't see the sister. It's not…it's not convenient.'

'Right,' said June, obviously thinking that everything wasn't right.

Angel half ran back to her room. There was no way she could get out of the ward. Perhaps he might see the baby then leave. She was hyperventilating, her chest heaving with the unaccustomed stress. She needed to calm down. He might just go.

After ten minutes she was allowing her hopes to rise. Perhaps he had seen the baby and left. Then there was a bang on her door, it flew open and the man stood outlined there. A tall man, casually dressed in jeans and sweater, with longish dark hair that needed brushing.

For a moment there was silence. Then he said, 'It's no good hiding. You knew I'd get to talk to you, didn't you?'

She was all right now. The fear had gone, there was only a cold anger. 'Yes, I guessed you might. And you know the reception you're going to get.'

'When I asked who was in charge your nurse said it was Angel—the sister. I couldn't believe it so I asked her to describe you.'

'That nurse could have answered all your questions. Please, sit down. Now you're here there's some paperwork we have to—'

'Paperwork! I didn't come here to...'

'I said sit down! I'm in charge of this ward now and, doctor or not, if you cause me any trouble I shall have absolutely no hesitation in sending for Security and having you thrown out. You know that, don't you?'

She could tell what an effort it cost him to contain his anger. But somehow he did it, sat in the chair she pointed to. 'Yes, I'm only too well aware of what you can do. Angel, I—'

'Angel is the name for my friends. In here I am Sister Thwaite. "Sister" will do if you have to call me anything.'

'Sister it shall be.' He appeared to have regained control of his temper. She knew this was when he was most dangerous.

'Mr Gilmour, first of all may I say how sorry we all are about the death of your sister. I didn't know that...' She caught herself, she should stick to being professional. 'I'm sure everything possible was done for her at A and E. If you wish, you could talk to Dr Croll. I gather he was her doctor when she was brought in.'

'I've already spoken to Dr Croll.' He pressed his hands to his face, as if he were trying to rub the tiredness away. 'My sister and I were estranged for all of our lives. Now there's no chance for us ever...I'm sorry, I mustn't burden you with my problems. Tell me about the little girl.'

Angel felt a fleeting touch of pity for him, knew she had to fight it down.

'Of course. The baby was born by Caesarean section. She's premature, about thirty-four weeks, and presented us with considerable problems, as I'm sure you gathered from seeing her. But for the moment the paediatric consultant thinks she's holding her own. Do you know what the baby was to be called?'

'I've no idea. I haven't seen my sister for fifteen years.'

'I see. Then you have no idea about her present address, where we might find her husband or partner? Are there any other relatives?'

'My sister was what they call "of no fixed abode" and there are no other relatives but me. I gather her partner disappeared the moment she told him she was pregnant. If you do find him, tell me. I'd like to come down and break his neck.'

'I'm sure you would. So you are the baby's only relation to come forward—her guardian. Do you want to come with me to see her?'

'I have seen her and I'm lost. I'm a cardiac specialist, all babies look the same to me.'

'She's tiny but she's perfect, a lovely baby,' Angel said. 'She is a person Mr Gilmour, she needs love from the minute she's born.'

'Don't we all?' he growled.

He looked at her. She reddened under his gaze, then fought back. 'Yes, we all need love. And consideration.'

The anger seethed between them. Perhaps it was a good thing when June looked in and said, 'Shall I get coffee?'

'No,' said Angel.

'Yes, please,' said Mr Gilmour.

They spoke at exactly the same time.

'Fetch two,' Angel said reluctantly. 'Mr Gilmour is helping me with some background queries.'

After a moment's silence, he said, 'It was a shock, finding you here. You were the last person I expected to meet. The last I heard, you were running a nursing station in the mountains of South America.'

'I was there for four years. Then I came home for good. My father is dead, my mother needs me and I love this place. This is where my roots are.' She caught herself. 'Not that it is any of your business.'

June came back with the coffee, and as they drank Angel reached for the forms she knew had to be handed in. 'You're a surgeon—you know that we have to fill in all these forms. I'll take what details you can give me, and forward them to anyone else who is concerned. We don't want to cause you too much pain. You understand that the police will want to speak to you? This was originally a traffic accident.'

'I've already made a short statement to them.'

'Good. The baby is quite premature, and prems always give cause for alarm. She will need to stay here in Intensive Care for a while, and then I suspect a week or two in the post-natal ward. Are you married, Mr Gilmour?'

'No, I am not married—not now.' The words were spoken with emphasis.

'Then I expect that all the arrangements for her posthospital care will have to be left to you, though we will have to inform Social Services. She will probably need reasonably competent nursing for a few months after she's discharged. As I said, you are her guardian.'

It appeared that this was a new idea to him. 'Of course,' he muttered. 'I'm her only relation. All she's got now is me. But I don't know how to look after a baby! I'm only here for six months then I'm taking up a post in central London. I hadn't heard from my sister for years when she phoned me last week. I didn't even know she was pregnant. I only knew that she had come to visit me when they rang through a couple of hours ago from A and E. They'd found my name and address in her purse.'

Angel hadn't realised that, and for a moment he had her sympathy. 'Oh, Mike, that must have been a shock! You never mentioned you had a sister!' She reached over, touched his arm.

'We were brought up separately. When I was younger I tried to get to know her, wrote to her and so on but it never worked.' Then he looked down at her hand. 'Sympathy?' he asked.

'For anyone who's had a loss.'

'What about sympathy for anyone who suddenly acquires an unexpected child?'

Before she could answer, June appeared. 'Sorry, Angel, but if you've a minute I'd like you to look at the monitor for baby George. BP seems just a bit low and—'

'I'll come at once, June. Will you take Mr Gilmour to see the new admittance again? Then see him out and report back to me. Mr Gilmour, I'll forward your name to all the other concerned parties. I'm afraid there'll be rather a lot of sorting out to do. And could you give us a name for the baby?'

'A name? I'm to choose a name?'

'Who else? Apparently you're her only relative. The staff here like babies to have names. It makes their charges more real, like proper human beings.'

'A name. What should I call it? Perhaps…'

'She's not an it, Mr Gilmour. She's a she.'

'Of course. My mistake. Very well, you may call her Suzanne.'

'Suzanne?' Angel paled, as if she had been struck. Suzanne was her own middle name. He was playing mind games with her.

'Suzanne sounds a very good name to me. It's honest and reliable and it will go well with Gilmour. Suzanne Gilmour. It's got a ring.'

He stood to follow June down the corridor. At the door he turned and said, 'You don't need to worry about the…about Suzanne, Sister. It's come as a shock but she's my responsibility now and I'll do all I can for her.' Then he was gone.

Angel went to look at baby George, decided that nothing much was wrong but that she would change him. There was comfort in handling the tiny body, following the well-known procedures. This was a part of the job she loved.

But her emotions were in turmoil. Still, she could take it, she was tough. Life in South America had taught her that. And other things had made her tough, a small voice reminded her.

When she had finished she saw June outside the room and beckoned her in. 'Has Mr Gilmour gone?' she asked.

'Not yet. He's standing by the incubator, staring down as if he doesn't know quite what to do.' June giggled. 'He asked quite a lot of questions about you, Angel—you know, casually, but it was obvious what he was doing. Said there was no wedding ring on your finger. D'you think he fancies you?'

'I doubt it. And nothing on this earth would make me go out with him.'

June looked surprised at Angel's outburst. 'I think he's nice. He's got a fit body and those blue eyes, and the way he smiles…not that he smiles very often.'

'It's what's inside a person that counts,' said Angel. 'If he asks for me again, say I'm busy with one of the other babies.'

In fact, this was true. The readings on baby George's monitor had continued to fall. Angel decided to call for the SHO. She still wasn't too worried, but rules dictated that a doctor had to be called. And she wanted to be certain so she rang through. Five minutes later Barry French ambled into her room, still rubbing his eyes.

Angel looked at him with vague affection. Barry was older than the average SHO, about her age. He had been a nurse before he trained to become a doctor, he knew how nurses felt. 'Problems with baby George?' he asked.

'You asked to be kept informed, so this is me informing you. I suspect it's nothing but I want you to make that decision.'

'OK, I'll take a look.'

So they looked at baby George together, and decided that as yet there was no real call for alarm. 'Don't forget,' he said, 'I don't really need sleep. You phone me and I'll be here.'

'Keen, alert and yawning like mad,' she said. 'Want a drink before you go back to bed?'

'Might as well. I'm not going to sleep for a while.' So they sat, drinking tea and talking idly in her room. After the confrontation with Mike it was restful. There was no need to shout, no need to take care with every word in case something was said that shouldn't have been said.

'Doing anything special on Saturday night?' he asked casually after a while. 'Fancy a meal or something somewhere?'

She thought about it for a minute. Over the past few weeks she'd realised he had been trying to decide whether to ask her out. He was basically a shy young man. Her first intention had been to say no—now she wondered why.

‘Why not ask June out there?’ she suggested. ‘She’s unattached and you could have a good time with her.’

‘Hmm,’ he said judiciously. ‘I’m not exactly looking for a good time, whatever that is. I just want to get to know you better. A lot of the time you seem a bit...reserved.’

‘I probably am,’ she said. ‘But, yes, Barry, I’d love to come out with you. Shall we sort out the details later? You’re probably too tired to make decisions about your social life now.’

‘I think you’re right.’ Barry unfolded himself from his seat. ‘Really looking forward to it, Angel. Oh! Can we help you?’

Angel looked up, behind her. Mike was in the doorway. She wondered how long he had been there, how much of the conversation he had heard. Had he heard Barry ask her out? Well, what she did was no concern of his!

‘Just to say that I’m going now. Sister, thanks for your help. I’m sure we’ll meet again soon.’

‘Probably not,’ she said stiffly. ‘I’ll be working nights for a while. Most arrangements will have to be made in the daytime.’

'Of course. Goodnight, then.' And he was gone.

Barry turned to her, lifted his eyebrows in enquiry. 'Brother of that woman who died after the car crash,' she explained, 'and apparently only relation of the little girl we admitted to come forward. He's a surgeon here.'

'Poor devil. There's going to be a lot of work for him.' Then Barry, too, was gone.

Half an hour later June also came in, for a well-earned break. 'Been a busy night,' she said. 'I still think that doctor fancies you. Asked even more questions.'

'He's just nervous,' Angel said, 'not sure how he'll cope with his new family.' In fact, she knew that somehow he would cope very well. He always did. She wondered if he would keep quiet about her or if it would suit him better to let everyone know. Perhaps not. Or perhaps tomorrow, when she came in for her night shift, all of the hospital would know that seven years ago, for nine brief months, Angel Thwaite had been married to Mike Gilmour, the new Cardiac surgeon.

The temperature in the neonatal unit was kept very high—certainly it was a little too warm to work in comfortably. Angel changed into her outdoor clothes, walked quickly down the corridor and out into the freezing early morning. The biting wind shocked her—but it revived her as well. From the moors above came the smell of wet heather. She loved it.

Behind her was the grey stone mass of Micklekirk Hospital. Built in the nineteenth century and built to last. Round the back there were new, sometimes portable buildings, all the necessities for a large regional hospital. But when she thought of where she worked, Angel always thought of this frontage.

Micklekirk itself was only a small town. The hospital served much of the country area not covered by Carlisle on one coast or Newcastle-upon-Tyne on the other. There were other small towns, villages, farms without number. Angel loved the area. This was where she belonged.

Ten minutes' drive from the hospital was the village of Laxley. It was the nearest place to Angel's home. She had been christened in the parish church, taught in the village school. It was a lively village—not pretty enough to attract large numbers of visitors, but deeply loved by most of its inhabitants.

Angel turned right out of the main street and after a hundred yards pulled up outside a stone bungalow. Valley View it was called, and outside was a FOR SALE sign. Angel pulled up her coat collar, got out of the car and walked to the end of the road. Beyond was the valley—a vista of fields, little farms, grazing sheep. Valley View would suit Angel and her mother very well—if they could afford it.

She was driving back to the main street when she saw an older woman waving vigorously to her. Annie Blackett. Angel knew her quite well.

'We've just sent Jackie off in the ambulance,' Annie said breathlessly. 'I've got a few things to do and then I'll go down to see her. They say it'll be a while before the baby comes.'

Angel looked at the tired face smiling down at her. 'Jackie will be all right,' she said. 'I'm not on her ward but tonight I'll drop in and see how she's getting on. Be good for her to see a familiar face.' She paused a moment and then asked, 'How's Terry managing?'

'Not well. I think prison is worse for him than it is for most people. But I tell him, he did the crime, now he must pay for it.'

'Will they let him out to see the baby?'

'I think so. There's some sort of new release system operating. He's been out once to see Mr Martlett at Brock Farm. He's offered Terry a job as a shepherd and a cottage when he gets out.'

'That'll be good for him. And Terry can do anything with animals. Mr Martlett will get a good worker. I can remember Terry in Miss Beavis's class in primary school, he used to help me with painting.'

'He's doing a lot of it now. Says it calms him down. I hope so. Bye, Angel. You look as if you need a sleep!'

Angel sighed and drove on. Terry Blackett in prison! He wasn't a bad lad, just not used to large numbers of people. They upset him, confused him. He'd got mixed up with some people from the coast, something to do with handling stolen cars, and the police had caught him. Handling cars! Terry was the was the best animal handler for miles. His girlfriend, Jackie Taylor, was pregnant. She'd been living for a while with Terry's mother. And in time Terry would come out, marry Jackie, take on the cottage and the sheep and be happy. A local problem, a local solution. People would cope.

She drove through Laxley, up onto the high moors road. Here the wind tore across the flattened grass, shaking her car. It nearly always did in winter. This was cold, bleak country. And then up ahead she saw a blackened stone building, seemingly huddled against the winds that tore at it. High Walls Farm. The place she lived.

The warmest room was the kitchen, and there she found her mother, waiting as usual with a hot meal. 'Ma! I do wish you'd stay in bed, look after yourself a little!'

'I'm fine. And if you're to work all night there's no way I'll let you cook your own breakfast.'

'I'm young and I'm strong and I haven't got a heart condition. You've remembered your pills?'

'If I didn't you'd soon let me know. Yes, I've taken them all. Be glad when I don't have to bother! Now, this afternoon, I can take the bus and—'

Angel put down her knife and fork with a crash. 'No, Ma! You're going for your appointment and I'm coming with you. We go in my car. No argument. Don't spoil my breakfast by trying.'

Marion Thwaite looked at her daughter fondly. 'Sometimes you remind me of me,' she said.

Fifteen minutes later Angel was in bed, giving thanks for the invention of electric blankets but still clad in a set of fleecy pyjamas. There was no heating on the top floor of High Walls. She was tired, but there was still time for a moment's worry.

Her mother had mitral stenosis, a heart condition brought on by rheumatic fever when she was seventeen and then a long hard life in an unforgiving climate. The cardiologist had said that an operation was inevitable—probably an artificial valve would be fitted. He would refer her to a surgeon but afterwards she must have an easier life. No way could she stay in High Walls. Everyone knew that. The difficulty was persuading her mother to move. Angel had hoped to move to Valley View, the bungalow in Laxley. But worryingly, they couldn't quite afford Valley View and Angel hadn't been able to find anywhere else.

Just as she was going to sleep something else struck Angel, something she should have thought of before. As the new cardiac surgeon, Mike was the man she would meet tomorrow with her mother. Her mother had never known about Angel's all too brief marriage. At the time she'd had problems of her own. More trouble!

Angel slept then, and had odd dreams of the past.

CHAPTER TWO

'THE leaflets in this section aren't very interesting,' Marion Thwaite said cheerfully. 'The last hospital I visited had little books warning me about diseases I'd never heard of and sexual practices that I would have thought impossible. This place is very boring. Just leaflets about diet.'

'Hush, Ma,' Angel scolded. 'Not everyone has your sense of humour. This waiting room isn't so bad.'

She supposed that all visits to a hospital involved waiting—certainly her own unit was no different from any other. But Micklekirk had decided that if waiting was necessary, it could at least be made comfortable. She sat with her mother in a very pleasant area, with a television set, not playing too loudly, a pile of newish magazines and papers and a small coffee-bar down the corridor. It could have been a lot worse.

Angel had asked the receptionist—yes, there was a new surgeon, yes, he was Mr Gilmour. So be it. She had never doubted Michael's skills as a doctor. In fact, a part of her was very pleased that he was to be her mother's surgeon. She only hoped they wouldn't fight again.

She kept her eyes fixed on the door to his room. When the time came, she would walk in coolly, the professional to the end. So she was surprised and a little irritated when he walked down the corridor and came up behind her. 'Angel…that is, Sister Thwaite, what are you doing here?'

She stood, turned to look at him. Now he was every inch the professional. Under the white coat were dark suit trousers, gleaming shirt, college of surgeons tie.

'I'm here with my mother, Mr Gilmour. She's been referred to you by the hospital cardiologist who thinks she may need surgery.'

'Of course. Please, come into my room. I've just got a quick call and then I'll be with you.'

Angel would rather have waited outside, but he ushered them into his consulting room and then left. She looked round. Apart from the usual medical appliances and computer terminal, there were academic books, surgical magazines, filing boxes. There was one unusual feature, though—a whiteboard had been installed on one wall. But other than that, nothing to show the man's personality. This was the room of a man who didn't intend to stay long.

'Mrs Thwaite!' he came back in the room, file clutched under his arm. 'My name's Michael Gilmour. I'm a surgeon here. And I've already met your daughter.' There was no double meaning, no secret message for Angel. This was a simple statement of fact. 'First of all, Mrs Thwaite, I'm very happy for your daughter to stay here with you. But this is your decision. If you'd rather she waited outside then that's fine.'

'She's my daughter and a nurse. She can stay.'

'I'm glad you feel that way. Now, I know that every time you come here the doctor does the same things, so I'm going to as well. Just a quick examination.' He took the usual pulse, blood pressure, listened to the heart. Then he sat behind his desk, riffled through the file of notes in front of him.

'You must be tired of tests, Mrs Thwaite. I see you've had a chest X-ray, an electrocardiogram, an ultrasound echocardiogram and a coronary angiography.'

'Seems a lot of tests when all that appears to be wrong with me is that I get tired easily.'

'But you also suffer from dyspnoea—sometimes it's hard for you to breathe?'

'I can always sit down.'

'But I'll bet you don't. Do you?'

'Well, I have my work to do.'

You're fifty-five, you don't smoke and never have done, you drink alcohol in moderation and you've cut down on the salt in your diet.'

'My daughter insists I cut down on salt,' Marion said drily. 'Makes food seem tasteless.'

'I sympathise. According to this sheet you filled in, you don't overeat and I see you're quite thin. You've got ruddy cheeks, but in this case that's not a sign of a healthy life outdoors. You're a widow and you...live with your daughter. Any more children?'

'I have a son who lives down near London. He works very hard, but he keeps in touch.'

'You've never fancied living near him? Say, if your daughter got married, moved away?'

Was this a gentle dig? Angel wondered. She said, 'That's not likely to happen. I'm settled here.'

'And living near London would kill me,' her mother added.

'I see.' Mike turned the sheets in front of him. 'Dr Forrester, whom you saw last, has got quite a lot to say about where you both live—High Walls Farm. Tell me about it, Mrs Thwaite. Tell me about your life there.'

Angel had to admit that Mike was good at his job. He was drawing her mother out, making her talk about her early life as a teenager in Laxley. 'So, when you were seventeen you thought all you had was a sore throat? And since the family was busy, you didn't want to bother them. Only when you were really ill, had agonising joint pains, did they realise you'd got something very bad—rheumatic fever. Did you develop chorea—what's known as St Vitus' dance?'

'No. The doctor came out every day. He said it might develop but it didn't.'

'That's good. Now, tell me about your married life—you were married to a farmer?'

He got her to talk about life on the farm, the way she had tried to keep some of it going when her husband had died. And he learned about the winds that scoured the moors, the cold in winter, the fact that the house was almost impossible to heat and draught-proof.

'I know it isn't ideal. But it's my home, it's the Thwaite home. My husband, my mother and my grandmother all lived and died there.'

'I know it's been your home, Mrs Thwaite, but you're going to have to think very strongly about moving. You know your body can only take so much. How many times have you had bronchitis in the past ten years?'

Marion was silent, so Angel said, 'Nearly every winter, Mr Gilmour. And last year I found out that on occasion she was spitting blood.'

'Right.' He stood and went to the whiteboard, quickly drew a picture of a heart. 'What's wrong with you, Mrs Thwaite, is that this valve here—we call it the mitral valve because it looks a bit like a bishop's mitre—is not able to do its job properly. The opening here between the left atrium and the left ventricle can't open far enough. Now, one treatment would be to use a transatrial balloon catheter—to put something in the opening and try to force it open. However, I suspect that wouldn't do much good. What I'd like to do is replace the valve with an artificial one. Now, this is a serious operation. I have to tell you that it could go wrong. But the consequences of not having it could be far more serious. I'd like you to go away, think about it and then let me know.'

'I'll have the operation. I'm fed up of being tired all the time, of not being able to do things.'

Mike smiled. 'I'd still like you to talk to your son and daughter, perhaps have a word with your GP.'

'She'll have the operation,' said Angel. 'I think it's a good thing, so does my brother, so does the GP. We'd like it as soon as possible.'

'Very well. But if you have second thoughts, do let me know. Mrs Thwaite, we can see to your heart. But you must take things easy now and after the operation you mustn't go back to that house. You'll be weak for quite a while and, frankly, your body won't be able to stand it. D'you fancy some kind of retirement flat?'

'I'd rather die at High Walls than live in a town,' Marion said. 'But Angel's been on at me to move and we have something in mind.'

Mike looked at Angel. 'There's a bungalow for sale called Valley View, just up the road in Laxley,' she said. 'It would be perfect for us. Small garden, central heating, no stairs. No work at all in the house. We know all the neighbours, even the GP is handy. And my mother just has to do something. She used to be a children's nurse, but there are no children near High Walls. When she has recovered perhaps we could find her a small job in Laxley.'

'That sounds ideal,' said Mike. 'So will you buy this bungalow?'

Angel shrugged. 'We're having another look round at seven this evening. But the question is whether we can afford it. It's right at the top of our price limit.'

'That's something I can't advise you on. Right, Mrs Thwaite, I'm putting you on my list for an operation in the next three or four weeks. Carry on with your current tablets and we'll let you know the date well in advance.' He stood, leaned over to shake hands. 'Been good talking to you.'

Angel and her mother left. Just before Angel walked through the door, Mike caught her by the elbow. 'You do know that it's very important that your mother finds somewhere less stressful to live?'

'Yes, Mr Gilmour, I do know. Thank you for your concern.' She didn't want to stay and talk further to him.

They drove back up to High Walls. 'He seems a very nice man,' said Marion. 'Have you met him before?'

'I'm looking after his niece. He was in the department last night.' Angel didn't want to go into detail, she was still unsure about Mike Gilmour.

'Well, I liked him. He seemed more human than the others I've seen—although they were good, too.'

'He has what they call a good bedside manner,' Angel said heavily. She stopped in the old yard of High Walls, the wind buffeting her car. 'Now, I'm going back for another couple of hours' sleep before we go down to see Valley View. I'd sleep easier if I knew you weren't trying to clean round this place and cook for me.'

'I'll just do the kitchen,' Marion promised. 'I'll get you up about six. Shall I have something hot ready for you?'

'No, Ma. I just won't be hungry then.' Angel sighed. If there was work to be done, her mother would do it.

That evening, they wandered round the bungalow, thinking about colour schemes, wondering where their furniture would go. This place would suit them very well. The reason Marion liked it was that there was a conservatory overlooking the valley. Even in winter she could sit out and watch the changing scene below. But it was also centrally heated, double glazed and all on one floor. The rooms were large but not too large, easy to clean. And shops and friends were only a few yards away. It was perfect, Angel thought. It was also, out of a dozen places they had visited, the only place her mother would even consider moving to.

Someone rang the doorbell. The estate agent? No, he had given them the keys, told them to return them when they were ready. Frowning, Angel opened the front door and gasped at who was there. 'What d'you want here?' she asked. It was Mike Gilmour.

He smiled and took a step forward, and she was forced to let him in. 'I said this afternoon that your mother should move and you told me about this place. I thought I would call, tell you what I thought of it.'

'We don't need your approval to buy a house,' she hissed. She wondered what the real reason was for him being here. Had he come just to persecute her?

'I think it's very kind of Mr Gilmour to come and advise us,' her mother said placidly. 'Not every surgeon would do that.'

'If I'm doing anything extra, Mrs Thwaite, it's because Angel is doing something extra for me. I've got my niece in her ward. I know she'll get the very best of care and attention there.'

'She's also being looked after by many other equally dedicated nurses and doctors,' Angel snapped.

But now he was wandering round, chatting happily to her mother. 'Gas fired central heating—good. I've noticed more than a few round here are solid fuel. And what's this?' He opened a door at the far end of the central corridor.

Angel answered. 'The last owner had his father living with him. He built on this extension so the old man could live a partly independent life. There's a big living/bedroom, an *ensuite* bathroom and a separate entrance. I suspect we'd keep this closed off in winter.'

'I see.' He looked at Angel. 'You wouldn't try to live here yourself? Have some independence?'

'No, I want to live with my mother. I've been independent, been abroad, come back here and I love it. I doubt I'll ever move.'

'No well-paid job in London beckoning?'

'I wouldn't take it for double the salary. Anyway, Micklekirk is a very good hospital. It's well managed, well supported financially. I'm pleased to be here.'

She knew there was an undercurrent to his probing questions but she didn't yet know what he wanted. So she told him the truth about how she felt. Nothing would drag her away from Micklekirk hospital.

'Good. I like it when families can stay together.' He frowned. 'Though I must say that I didn't manage very well with my sister.' For a moment Angel thought she saw pain flicker in his eyes, but he went on, 'I hope you get this bungalow, I can't think of a better place for my patient to live. Are you going back home now up to—High Walls, was it?'

'For a bite of supper and then into work,' said Angel.

'Ah. I'm only staying at Micklekirk for six months so I've got myself a room in the residency. I usually dine in the hospital, which is quite good, but occasionally I need a change. Could I invite you two ladies to dinner at that pub in the main street? I've been told the food there is very good.'

It happened again.

'No,' said Angel.

'Yes, please,' said her mother.

Then, when Angel hesitated, Marion said, 'Mr Gilmour has been very kind to us, Angel. The least we can do is accept his hospitality.' To Mike she said, 'You must come to tea soon, Mr Gilmour, if you're not too busy.'

'I should really enjoy that. Shall we go for a meal, then?' Apparently, they would.

Angel and Mike had a moment alone while her mother went to fetch her coat. 'Just what are you playing at, Mike?' Angel asked in a furious whisper.

He shrugged. 'Just trying to be helpful. And I really like your mother.'

She'd been in the Cat and Fiddle quite a lot through the years, and she recognised more than a few people there. Janet Card, a girl who had been in school with her, came over to sell some raffle tickets. 'They're trying to close the village school, you know. We're getting up a petition, forming a committee to fight the closure. Miss Beavis is the leader.'

'Miss Beavis! She must be in her late eighties!' Miss Beavis had been headmistress of the village school well before Angel's time. But then she had become a regular visitor and part-time teacher after she'd retired. Miss Beavis was formidable.

'She might be getting on, but she still stands for no nonsense,' said Janet. 'Will you come to a meeting once we've got all our support? We'll pass the word round when we've fixed a date.'

'I can try,' said Angel.

Since her mother was with them there was no need to worry—if Angel had been on her own with Mike there might have been gossip. But her mother and Mike seemed to get on well. Angel was the one left out of the conversation.

The food at the Cat and Fiddle was supposed to be very good, but afterwards Angel couldn't remember what she had eaten. She still wondered what Mike was doing here—and she was still nervous in his presence. He seemed to have got over yesterday's bewilderment and Angel couldn't tell if he was intent on charming Marion or was being charmed by her.

When they parted both Marion and Mike said that they must meet again. Angel's views weren't asked.

'Seems a very nice man, Angelina,' said Marion. She was the only one occasionally to use Angel's full name. 'Why don't you go out more often? Meet more young men? You know, I loved being married.'

'Well, I'm married to my job,' said Angel. 'And, anyway, on Saturday I'm going out with a young doctor from my ward.'

'That'll be very nice,' Marion said placidly.

That night she was working with June again. At handover they had been told that things were normal—baby George had made slight progress but baby Suzanne wasn't progressing as well as had been hoped. But there was nothing much to worry about.

For the first couple of hours Angel and June carried on with the normal work of the unit. They now had six babies there—three in cots, three in incubators. All were monitored, and they had to keep a close eye on the readings.

Baby George had at first been fed on demand, now he was fed every two hours. Angel took the cap from the tube that was taped to his face, ran through his nose and down to his stomach. With a small syringe she aspirated some of the baby's stomach contents, sucking a tiny amount up into the syringe. Good, she could tell that the milk was partly digested. She returned the contents of the syringe to the stomach, got a larger syringe and filled it with the fifteen mils of milk that George was entitled to. Then she took the plunger out of the syringe and let gravity feed the baby.

There was the baby-care routine before each feed. The eyes might need cleaning, the mouth wiped out with a damp cotton bud, perhaps a little petroleum jelly smeared on the lips. Then a quick temperature check before the nappy was changed.

It was routine work, but it was a routine that Angel loved. There was something satisfying about handling such tiny human beings. And they all had different characters.

Then there was a lull. It was too early to try to catch half an hour's sleep, so she told June where she would be, made sure she was carrying her bleep and walked out of her section and into the delivery suite. On one wall of the midwives' station was a big whiteboard with the names of the mums in labour, which room each was in and the progress they were making. Jackie Taylor was in room three, a rim of cervix showing, which meant that she would give birth at any moment. Angel frowned. It seemed rather a long time since this morning, it had been a long-drawn-out birth.

Work in the delivery suite was erratic. One night there might be a couple of births, the next night seven or eight. Tonight the midwives were busy. Angel thought she'd pop into room three and see how Jackie was doing.

'May I come in?' Angel could tell that the birth was imminent. Annie Blackett, Jackie's soon-to-be mother-in-law, was standing by the bed holding her hand. Both seemed happy to see Angel. And the midwife was most pleased of all. 'Angel, Jackie here is about to deliver—can you stay here ten minutes? There's no one else to help.'

'Happy to help out. If I'm bleeped I'll have to go back, but we should be OK for a while.'

'Ten minutes is all I need. Bless you. Now, Jackie, push!' Angel knew that seeing a familiar face, having an ordinary conversation, was often the best way of coping with pain and exhaustion. As the birth progressed she chatted to Jackie and Mrs Blackett about the future.

'They think that Terry will be allowed out to see the baby,' Jackie gasped. 'You don't know how keen he is to see it. Funny for a man, isn't it?'

'Not for Terry. He's always loved babies. That's why he's such a good animal man. He thinks giving birth is wonderful.'

'I...wish...he was here with me.'

'I'm sure he does, too. But it won't be long now, Jackie. Just concentrate on pushing and... It's a little girl!'

As second in the room, Angel was to take the baby. The midwife cut the cord, Angel wrapped up the little girl, took her to the cot and gave her the regulation baby check—just a quick inspection to see if there were no obvious flaws, a finger in the mouth to check for the palate, a hand run up and down the spine. When a husband or partner was present Angel liked to do the check with him. But, of course, Terry was in prison.

Then the little girl was laid on her mother's breast.

Angel filled in the Apgar form, giving a score of nine out of ten. A good baby, Terry and Jackie could be proud.

Then her bleep went.

'Thanks a lot, Angel,' the midwife said. 'Made it easier for all of us.'

'My pleasure. Jackie, I'll be in again to see you, but that's a darling baby. Don't let Terry spoil her!'

She trotted down the corridor to the nearest phone. 'Angel here, June. What's the problem?'

'Well, Mr Gilmour's here again and he's not very happy that I'm the only one in charge. He wants to know when you're coming back and says your place is here.'

'Anything wrong with any of the babies?'

'Nothing at all. They're all fine. You know I'd have bleeped you.'

'Of course. On my way back, June.'

She walked smartly down the corridor, tapped in the code to let her into the unit, moved to the room where baby Suzanne was lying. Mike was there, scowling down at the tiny pink figure. 'Sister, I thought your place was here with your charges, not wandering round the building, looking up old friends.'

What a change from the way he had spoken to her not four hours ago! She ignored him, checking the monitors of each of the babies in turn. Then she said, 'At present I'm in charge of this unit. If you have any objections to the way it is run, please, make them to the senior nursing officer. I will say that I have every confidence in Nurse Wright and that had there been any emergency I was two minutes' away. Now, how may I help you?'

He was angry again—it was too bad. She could see the glint in his eyes. She remembered how his lips tightened when he didn't get his own way. They tightened now. Then somehow he forced himself to relax. 'Angel, I—'

'I told you, visitors call me Sister.'

This angered him more than ever but no way was she going to back down. Finally, he said, 'Sister, then. Might I have a report on the progress of my niece?'

'Certainly. I have her notes here. During the day she was visited by Linda Patterson, the paediatric consultant, and this is the course of treatment she has prescribed.'

'I see.' He took the notes, leafed through them. 'It looks like she's going to make a complete recovery.'

'We hope so. But even when she's discharged she'll need nursing care for a few months. She'll need... Have you any plans for her future yet?'

'None at all yet,' he said sombrely 'It's hard to call someone a problem when she's so small and helpless, but I'm afraid she is. What would you do with an un—an unexpected child?'

'I do hope you weren't going to say "unwanted child". It's not my place to advise you what to do. I can only tell you what I wouldn't do—I wouldn't even think of abandoning the child.'

'Very noble. Rest assured, nothing will make me abandon Suzanne, Sister. And I take it you only abandon those old enough to look after themselves? In spite of any promises you might have made?'

'No, Mr Gilmour, I only abandon those so selfish that they think no one but them matters. Is there anything else?' She held out her hand for the sheaf of notes.

'Nothing else, thank you. I leave the child in your very capable hands. Goodnight, Sister. And let me say again that Suzanne will have as happy a life as I can give her and I have no intention of abandoning her.'

June came into the room when she saw Mike leave. 'Why does he always look angry when he talks to you, Angel? You don't irritate any of the other parents—you're good with them.'

'Mr Gilmour is different to all the other parents, June. Very different.'

It happened, as it so often did, in the bleakest hour of the night. Baby Suzanne had her antibiotics and seemed to be happy. But then the alarm on her monitor sounded. The oxygen saturation level was down and there was a dusky look round Suzanne's mouth.

The first thing to do was check the endotracheal tube to make sure that the oxygen mix was reaching the baby. Angel tried suction, the tube was clear. When the saturation level continued to sink Angel rang Linda, at present in the Residency.

'Increase the oxygen,' Linda said with a yawn, 'and ring me straight back. I'm not going to sleep now.' Angel increased the oxygen as she'd been told, then phoned Linda back.

'Saturation level still going down and she's looking even duskier. Heart rate isn't looking good either.' It wasn't Angel's job to diagnose, but this was a job she knew well. 'I think she's blown a pneumothorax.'

'Get the cold light out. I'll be there in five minutes.'

Angel suspected that air was escaping from one of Suzanne's lungs into the pleural cavity, the space round the lungs. This had collapsed the lung—and Suzanne needed all the lung capacity she could get.

When Linda arrived Angel handed her the cold light—in effect, an intensely powerful torch that would shine its beam right through a baby's body. All other lights in the room were switched out. Then Linda directed the beam at Suzanne's chest and it revealed what Angel had suspected. A dark shadow showed that one lung had collapsed.

There was no time to confirm by X-ray. Linda at once put in a chest drain, sliding a thick needle into the pleural cavity and then suturing it in place. The needle was connected to a flutter valve, and the two watched as the air started to drain from the pleural cavity.

Suzanne's lung should now reinflate. But had the shock been too much for her? Her heart rate and the oxygen saturation level continued to go down.

Ideally the heart rate should have been about 130 to 140 beats per minute. It was now below a hundred. The oxygen saturation level had dropped from near a hundred to seventy-two. And still both sank.

June had phoned Barry as she knew Linda would want his presence. He, too, examined the tiny form and read the notes as Linda, June and Angel looked on. Even at this stage Linda remembered that she was supposed to be a teacher. 'What do you think is the right thing to do, Barry?'

He thought. 'We've just been hoping she's strong enough to survive. Now that doesn't seem very likely. But I can't see any treatment or any medication working.'

'I agree entirely. Angel, isn't the guardian a surgeon here? Perhaps you ought to get him down.'

'I'll see to it straight away.' She walked to her office. This kind of thing happens, she told herself. It's no fault of ours, it happens. We did everything possible for the little mite, now she has to fight on her own. I've got to be professional—be caring but be detached as well. But it was hard. She had taken to Suzanne, the little girl deserved some good luck.

She had Mike's internal number on her desk and she phoned before thinking about what she was to say to him. On the second ring the phone was picked up and a sleepy voice said, 'Mike Gilmour here. This is a terrible hour to call a man.'

For a moment seven years were swept away and she was back in a time when things had been so different, when she had been so happy. No matter how little sleep Mike had had, he had always been able to wake good-humoured. It was a trait she envied. Before she could stop herself she said, 'Come on, sleepyhead, you have to wake up.'

'Angel?' Only her name and yet in the way he spoke it she could read... Nothing, she decided. She had to remember who he was, why she was calling. There was no other possible emotional relationship between them.

'I'm very sorry to have to call you, Mr Gilmour. I'm afraid Suzanne has taken a turn for the worse. Perhaps you ought to come down quite quickly.'

There was a silence and she wondered what he was thinking. When he spoke again his voice seemed to be entirely neutral. But Angel had once lived with him, she could feel the emotion under the iron control. 'You don't think she's going to make it?'

'We can't possibly tell, but she is very ill.' The next question was one she hated asking but it had to be done. 'Would...would you like me to make arrangements to have her christened? Before...in case it's too late?'

Now he was fully awake, his tone metallic. She remembered that tone so well. It was the way he sounded when he was going to do whatever was necessary, no matter what it cost. It was a tone that had always upset her. Why couldn't he give way, why couldn't he show what he was feeling? But it was now no business of hers.

'It might be a good idea. I've no idea what her mother was, but I'm C. of E. I'd like her to be christened into that church. I'll be there in five minutes.'

The hospital had an arrangement with the vicar of Laxley, who was the hospital chaplain. Angel phoned him at once. He, too, was accustomed to being called out at night. She told him what was happening, a little about Mike and the baby. Then she went back to the incubator room. They had other charges that had to be fed, changed and checked. For them life was going on. Angel found that working calmed her. Nothing was worse than just standing, watching, hoping.

Mike came down. Angel left it to the consultant to introduce herself, to explain what was happening. Then, when the Reverend Whitby came in, she took him in to meet the others. She liked Eric Whitby. He was a cheerful, hard-working man, who had given up a well-paid job as a solicitor to become a clergyman.

'Mr Gilmour, this is the Reverend Eric Whitby.'

Only then did Angel realise what Mike was going through. He stared at Eric as if he had just realised why he was there. For a moment

Mike couldn't speak, then she saw him take a great breath, saw his shoulders hunch and then relax.

Mike's face was completely impassive as he shook hands. 'I'm sorry you have to be dragged out at night, Reverend.'

What an empty thing to say, Angel thought, but she understood Mike's desperate state of mind, and she knew that Eric did, too.

Eric smiled. 'You're a surgeon, and I'm sure this has happened to you. Being called out is nothing when we think of the reasons for it.'

Mike rubbed his face. Angel remembered how he used to do that when he was tired or upset. He wouldn't say anything—just rubbed his face. Deliberately repressed memories flashed through her mind. Irritated, she shook her head. This was a time for work, not reflection.

'I should know that,' Mike now confessed. 'In a lot of my cases I've noticed that when people are really…concerned, they worry about the most trivial things. I don't like it when it happens to me. But I'm this little girl's only relation, and it's come as a shock.'

Eric reached out, rested his hand on Mike's shoulder a moment. Then he became business-like. 'I don't want to interfere with any medical procedures. There's a special service for cases like this so I'd like to baptise this child, say a quick prayer, and then, if you'd like to talk to me, Mr Gilmour, I'll stay with you as long as you wish.'

From his bag he took a silk stole, draped it round his neck. This, Angel knew, was his badge of office. 'I take it there has been no time to find godparents?'

'I'm not Suzanne's father, I'm her uncle,' said Mike. 'I want to be her godfather.'

'I'll be godmother if I may,' said Angel. 'I've only known her a few hours but I've got very fond of Suzanne.' It seemed terribly sad that a two-day-old child had so few friends, so few people who cared for her.

'If you wish to, I'd like that,' said Mike.

The service was swift. Then Linda Patterson said she would go as there was nothing more she could do. Barry said he would stay a while longer. 'Would you like to talk?' Eric asked Mike. 'Sometimes it helps. At other times I know people want to be left to themselves.'

'It's very kind of you to ask, but I think I'd like to stay here, wait and see what happens. I have some thinking to do.'

No one seemed to want to leave the room. Mike, Angel, Barry and Eric all stood and gazed at the little white-swathed figure, the tiny pink face, the almost imperceptible rise and fall of the chest. Then they would look at the monitor, watch the tell-tale trace of the oxygen saturation level. This was the most reliable guide to Suzanne's progress. It was still dropping. All of them knew what it meant—Eric had asked for the equipment to be explained to him when he'd first started this job.

Over the past hour that trace had descended from 95 to its present 60. If it continued its downward path, in another half-hour Suzanne would be dead.

Sixty…59…58…57… A small life, trickling away, marked by an electronic monitor. For a mad moment Angel thought that it was the monitor that was killing the child, forcing the take-up rate to slow. Then she bit her lip, pressed her fingernails into her palms. The pain brought her round. Such thoughts were not suitable for a nurse!

Fifty-seven...57...58... No one commented. Fluctuations like this were not uncommon. Fifty-nine...60...61... Then quickly, 64...69...

The tension in the room was palpable; this kind of recovery could happen—but it was very rare. At 69 the rate of increase slowed, the level dropped...68...67...but then it accelerated again and within two minutes the indicator read 90.

Angel looked at the set faces staring downwards. She could tell what Barry was thinking, what June was thinking, what Eric was thinking. Only Mike remained stone-faced. Hadn't he yet learned that letting your emotions show was not a sign of weakness? To her his suffering was obvious; she wondered if it was to the others.

It wasn't good just to stand there. Angel took Barry and Eric to her room for coffee. The alarm on Suzanne's monitor was, of course, set and June was in the room, but Mike, his face still completely impassive, said he would stay by the incubator. Angel remembered that expression well. When Mike wanted to hide his thoughts, he could do so better than anyone she knew. But then she noticed his hands, gripping the rail of the incubator. The knuckles were white. He might not be willing to demonstrate what he was feeling—but he was certainly feeling something. Angel felt a pang of pity for the solitary figure.

Coffee was welcome. After the drama they all felt the need for something calming, soothing. 'That was a very heartening experience,' Eric said. 'I've never seen anything like that before and it made me feel…' obviously he was looking for the right words '…both humbled and grateful. I couldn't ask out there—but what are baby Suzanne's chances of survival now?'

Barry shrugged. 'Who can tell? I would say pretty good, there's no reason why this improvement shouldn't continue. And don't anyone tell me that medicine is an exact science, it isn't.'

'Nothing to do with human beings is exact,' said Eric, 'I know that. D'you think Mr Gilmour will be all right on his own? Should I take him a coffee?'

'He'll be fine on his own,' said Angel, and was conscious of the other two looking at her, wondering why she spoke with such certainty. To change the subject, she asked, 'How d'you find doctors as patients, and as parents of patients Barry?'

'Terrible,' Barry said. 'They always know too much about medicine in general, and not quite enough about this particular branch of medicine. I know we're supposed to keep patients informed—but I'm a doctor, not a lecturer.'

The other two laughed. There was still tension in the room but they were slowly feeling easier.

'So Mr Gilmour is a surgeon here?' asked Eric, 'I didn't know that. He seemed very composed, but I suspect he wasn't.'

'I was chatting to him in the doctors' lounge,' Barry said. 'He's done some high-powered work in America. Unfortunately he won't be here for long, there's a post he's been promised in London. It's a pity, there aren't many first-class heart surgeons around and we've got plenty of call for one here in Micklekirk. A man could build a reputation up here.'

'Perhaps he prefers the bustle of London to the peace of Micklekirk,' said Angel. 'I know which I'd rather have.'

She looked up as someone knocked on the door then opened it. It was Mike. 'Is everything all right?' she asked anxiously.

'Everything is fine. Suzanne continues to improve and, as you once told me, June Wright is a more than competent nurse. I'm hopeful now and it's a good feeling.' He stepped into the small room and suddenly Angel felt that it was getting overcrowded. 'I'd better soon be back in bed. I've got a full list tomorrow and I can't let those patients suffer. But I wondered if I could beg a coffee.'

Angel poured him one, strong, black and sugarless, handed it over with the words, 'Just as you like it.' Then she flinched again. How was she supposed to know that? But no one seemed to notice her little mistake.

'We've been hearing that you've worked in the States, Mr Gilmour,' Eric said conversationally. 'Coming to Micklekirk must be quite a culture shock.'

'After New York, Boston and Chicago, it is a bit of a change. But there are compensations.'

Did he glance at her as he said that?

'And does American medicine differ much from our home-grown version?'

Angel knew what Eric was doing. Mike had suffered a traumatic experience—perhaps they all had—and after such a thing there was nothing better than to be forced to return to ordinary, everyday life. This was the kind of question Mike would get all the time. It would do him good to have to answer. But she suspected that he also knew what Eric was trying to do.

Mike thought for a minute. 'Technically, America is a little ahead of us,' he said. 'Over there I get more time and more funding for my work so perhaps my results are better. But I still think the British National Health Service, with all its faults, is the best system in the world.'

She couldn't help it. 'And yet you spent seven years abroad away from it?' she snapped.

'Personal reasons,' he said smoothly. 'Thanks for the coffee, Sister. I'd better get to bed.' At the door he turned. 'Barry, Sister here told me last night that when Suzanne recovers, she'll be able to go home but that she'll require quite intensive care.'

'Probably,' said Barry. 'It's early days yet, but I think at least her first year will be difficult. After that she should be fine.'

'What'll be best for her is a loving, caring family,' said Angel.

'A loving, caring family?' he said thoughtfully. 'A pity you can't get that on prescription. I'll say goodnight to Suzanne and go to bed. You won't hesitate to phone me if...'

'We'll phone you,' said Angel.

Her other two visitors left shortly afterwards and Angel and June continued with their tasks—the feeding, observations, drugs. As ever, the familiar routine calmed Angel, reasserted her confidence. She was Angel Thwaite, a competent children's nurse, doing what she knew and liked.

Just before handover the next morning, June called her to the phone. It was Mike, asking about Suzanne.

'Much much better,' said Angel. 'It's up to the doctors to say, of course, but I would think that she's definitely on the mend.'

'Good. I'll drop in to see her at lunchtime. Are you in again tonight? Start at nine-thirty?'

'Yes. It'll be the third night of my five-night rotation.'

'I see.' There was a pause, and when he spoke she could hear the doubt in his voice. 'Angel, I'd like to meet you to chat for an hour or so before you start work. Not in the hospital—somewhere on what we might call neutral ground.'

'Meet you? Why? Oh, just a minute.'

She turned and said, 'Go and check the readings on baby George, will you, June?'

June realised she was being dismissed and thought she knew why. She winked broadly at Angel as she left. Angel sighed. She could do without this.

'We haven't seen or heard from each other in seven years. Why bother trying to talk now?' she asked.

'Because it is seven years. We're both older, perhaps wiser. There are things we have to sort out.'

'But I still don't like you.'

Now she could hear the laughter in his voice. 'Fair enough. There are times when I'm not too fond of you. Still…can you remember anything good about the nine months we were together?'

She didn't know whether she ought to answer that question. But eventually she said. 'Yes, I remember quite a lot of good things.'

'Me, too. So meet me somewhere.'

She was going to say no, but somehow the answer came out the opposite. 'All right, then. But, understand, this is just to sort out how we work together. This is not the start of something new. We're a boring old story, everything between us is past. And I have a man in my life.'

'Ah. Let me guess, the lucky Dr Barry French. He seems a very able young man. Now, this is your area, you know the district—where shall we meet? I liked the Cat and Fiddle.'

'Not there. I don't want us to be seen by anyone who knows us, either from home or hospital.' She thought a minute. 'Five miles down the main road there's a big roadside pub called the Drovers' Arms. There's a quiet room at the back, we could meet there at about eight tonight.' If she had to meet him she wanted it over quickly.

'About eight tonight, that's fine. Will you have dinner with me?'

'No, I'll have eaten, just a fruit juice will do fine. This isn't a social occasion, it's just a meeting to get things sorted out.'

'What else?' he asked.

I'm not sure what I'm doing here, Angel thought to herself as she drove into the large car park of the Drovers' Arms. Her life recently had been happy. She had settled into living with her mother, enjoyed her work, was reasonably fulfilled. Once or twice she had been out with men but she had treated her affairs with caution. She didn't really need men. She'd had one and it hadn't worked out.

Mike was there already, watching for her, and he came out to meet her. A small courtesy but a thoughtful one. He escorted her to the quiet back room, fetched her a fruit juice and himself a beer. 'I've got exactly an hour,' she said, 'and I'm still not sure what I'm doing here.'

'I'm not sure either. But apparently, unlike you, I wanted to be here.'

She couldn't trust herself to contradict him. 'Why do you want to be here? Why do you want to talk to me?'

'Because the happiest time of my life was spent with you.'

This shook her. She was sure he was telling the truth, and knew that she had felt the same way. But that had been then. 'That time has passed,' she said. 'It passed after nine months.'

'Nine months out of a lifetime isn't long to be truly happy.'

'Perhaps you should have thought that before rushing off to America!' She was angry now. 'Mike, I don't need all this, it's a complete waste of time. We were married, we couldn't agree so we got divorced. In six months you'll be gone and I can get round to forgetting you again.'

She saw the tell-tale signs—the firming of his lips, the narrowed eyes. She had angered him, but somehow he kept control. 'There was so much between us,' he said. 'I remember it often, and even if it's now gone we should...celebrate what we had.'

Celebrate. It seemed an odd word to use. Rather than celebrate, she had tried to forget. 'Asking me to remember is hard,' she said. 'You risk making me lose my temper.'

He grinned. 'How well I know that. Do you remember telling that paediatric consultant that he might be a brilliant doctor, but that as a human being you'd seen better specimens in the zoo?'

She flushed. 'I'm older, I'm more controlled now.' She thought a moment about the incident he'd referred to. 'But I was right.'

'I suspect you were. And I also suspect you are more controlled now.' He seemed ill at ease, not sure of what he wanted to say.

She was uneasy herself, not knowing which way the conversation was going. She still didn't know what he wanted of her. More unsettling, she didn't know what she wanted of him. 'So why did you want to talk to me?' she asked flatly.

'Somehow we have to work together, not snarl each time we meet. Be friends even—in public at least. For a start, I'm going to have to make arrangements with you about your mother. Our personal feelings can't get in the way of our professional duties.'

'I can see that. All right, Mike, we'll both make an effort to get on.'

'Fine. Because I really like Marion. Right now I'm her surgeon, and that's the most important thing between us. But afterwards, when she's recuperated, I can see her becoming a friend.'

Angel looked at him anxiously. 'That might make things difficult.'

'It's that difficulty I'm trying to sort out now. The other thing, of course, is Suzanne. She's mine now, Angel, and I'm going to be as hard as any other parent, fighting for what's best for his child. You can help me—or help her—and I want to know that I can count on you.'

This was a new Mike, and one she rather liked. 'Of course you can,' she said. 'Apart from the fact that I'm getting rather fond of Suzanne myself, I suppose I owe you something.'

'Perhaps we owe each other something?'

She didn't want to go into that. She glanced at her watch. Time had passed far more quickly than she had thought. It was time to be professional now. 'Have you made any decisions about Suzanne?' she asked. 'And, incidentally, why did you choose that name?'

'I called her after you, of course,' he said. 'I could hardly have called her Angel, could I?'

'Why call her after me?'

He grinned. 'Because the two of you have caused me more trouble and more heartache than any other women I know. It's fitting that you should share a name. As to what to do about her, I just don't know yet. I want the very best for her, and I guess I want to share in her life. But she must have a happy childhood—happier than I ever had. I have to face up to my responsibilities and I'm not going to try to wriggle out of them.' He frowned. 'And I'm starting to...love her.'

'That's the word. And I'm very pleased you're going to look after her.' She still wasn't sure how she felt about him naming the child after her. 'Now, I must go, Mike, or I'll be late for work. I'm glad we've had this talk. Quite frankly, I didn't want it but I think we've got things sorted out. Incidentally, you haven't told anyone we were once married?'

'No. I thought you'd prefer not to.'

'Best for both of us, I think.' Together they stood and moved to the exit.

After the warmth of the hotel it was bitterly cold outside. She pulled her coat around her, slipped her hands into the pockets. He walked with her to her car, stood as she took out the key. They were in the shadow of a line of trees, well away from the neon-lit façade of the hotel.

She didn't know how or why it happened. Suddenly his arms were round her, pulling her to him, his mouth coming down onto hers. So unexpected was it that she responded at once. She held him as tightly as he held her, her lips parting willingly to his passionate kiss. It was a kiss that jerked back the happiest memories of her life, and yet seemed somehow new. She had been in love with a boy, but this was a man she was holding. His body was so close. She could remember… She wrenched herself away.

'Mike, that wasn't right! You shouldn't have done that!'

His reply was soft but fierce, as if each word was meant. 'Maybe I shouldn't have kissed you, but you enjoyed it as much as I did. Didn't you?'

'That's why it was wrong. There's nothing between us now, nothing at all.' Her sudden lapse had made her angry, she wanted him to know how furious she was. 'We've just had your quiet, civilised talk, trying to sort things out between us. I went along with it. But you'd better understand this, Mike, I don't feel quiet and civilised. You let me down. You betrayed me. You put your career before our relationship and that's why we got divorced and that's why I still don't like you.'

Before he could reply she was in the car, backing away so he had to move aside. As she moved out onto the road she glanced in her mirror. He was standing motionless where she had left him.

CHAPTER THREE

It was good to come off night shifts. There was the usual period when Angel's body wasn't sure whether it was day or night, but that was soon over. She would be on earlies or lates—mornings or afternoons—now for quite a while. Something to look forward to.

She enjoyed her evening out with Barry. He took her to the nearest big town, where they had dinner in a newly opened steakhouse and then went to a jazz club in the back room of a large pub. She was rather touched by that. Barry had heard her humming 'St Louis Blues' and had apparently casually asked her if she liked jazz. She had said she liked traditional jazz and so he had found a club where they could listen to it.

'You listened and then you went to that trouble just for me?' she asked. 'That was lovely of you.'

'No, just for me, Angel. I think you're well worth the trouble. And it's my training. You know that medicine largely consists of making lots of small observations.'

She sighed. 'I thought he was taking me out as a woman. And all he wants to do is make large numbers of small observations. I'm just a case to you, aren't I, Barry?'

'Much, much more than that,' he said, and though they were joking, she thought that she heard a thread of truth in his voice. She would have to be careful. She was very fond of Barry and didn't want to hurt him.

'I've really enjoyed myself. Shall we go out again soon?' he asked after he had driven her home.

'I've enjoyed myself, too. Yes, I'd love to go out again.' But when she got into the house she reminded herself that Barry would never be more than a friend—though a dear one. She would have to tell him that.

Next morning there was a letter with the heading of the estate agent. Excited, Angel tore it open. Perhaps their bid for the house had been accepted. But the news was bad. Feverishly, she read the three paragraphs again and again. 'Another offer...an extra three thousand pounds...would like to sell to you but must look after the interests of my client...happy to sell to you if you can match this...'

So that was the end of her dreams. There was no way she could claw together another three thousand pounds, she had gone far beyond her limit already. Now she would have to start again on the long dreary round of estate agents, looking for somewhere where her mother would be happy and that they could afford. Valley View would have been perfect! Angel said nothing to her mother, stuffing the letter into her briefcase.

She was feeling rather low as she walked down the corridor towards the neonatal ward, not paying much attention to the throng of parents, nurses and porters. Then she heard a voice shout to her, 'Hey, Angel.' She looked up. There was Terry Blackett.

He looked thinner, and paler than she'd ever seen him. There was an air of unease about him, as if he wasn't sure of his welcome here. But he was obviously pleased to see her, a familiar face.

'Terry! You've come to see your new baby? Isn't she lovely? You're a lucky lad.'

'Not that lucky, Angel. I'm on my way back now—they only let me out for a quick trip. But she's a lovely baby.'

'I've dropped in to see her now and then.' She looked at him. 'Will you be able to come regularly?'

His face now was grim. 'Not regularly. This is a new scheme, letting prisoners out so they can get used to life outside. But it only upsets me, Angel. Having to leave Jackie and the baby, and deliberately walk back into that place—you don't know what it takes.'

'I can guess, Terry. Now, look, the baby and Jackie are going to be fine, we'll keep an eye on them. Your mother says you've got another six months to go. Well, I know you're tough, you can do it. And you've got such a lot to look forward to!'

'I know that, Angel. It's the one thing that I think about. But that place...you're never on your own! Sometimes I need to be by myself, and there's nowhere.'

'You can do it! You've *got* to do it, you've got a baby to think of now!'

'I know.' He glanced at his watch. 'Better go. If I'm even five minutes late I don't get the chance again.'

'Just hang on, Terry. You'll be all right.'

There are people with bigger problems that me, she thought gloomily as she keyed in the code to the neonatal ward door. I hope Terry manages. She hadn't liked his air of quiet desperation. At school Terry had been a quiet, reasonably good child. But if he was pushed too far he could run riot.

Barry and Angel stood by the side of the incubator, looking at the little form below them. Suzanne was improving day by day. Her movements were stronger, her crying louder. She just looked a healthier baby.

'I think we can stop worrying about her now,' Barry said to her later. 'She's made good progress and her breathing and heart rate are both better than we might have thought. In a week or so I suspect we would be able to discharge her but we'll keep her in till she's nearly full term. She'll need quite intensive care for a while but she should be all right.'

'Who's going to look after her?' Angel asked, 'if Mr Gilmour is her only relation.'

Barry shrugged. 'I don't know. It's a bit difficult to say anything when the guardian is a colleague. But I guess he'll have to get in touch with Social Serviccs, see what they can do for him.'

'We do need the beds,' Angel said doubtfully. 'She can't stay here indefinitely.'

Usually, discharging a baby was a joy. She got fond of them, of course, it was hard not to have an emotional relationship with a baby who you had watched over and helped to fight its way through to health. But when she saw proud and happy parents carrying away a tiny bundle that she had nursed through to strength, she thought hers was the best job in the hospital. Discharging Suzanne would be different.

'D'you want to have a word with Mr Gilmour when he comes down?' asked Barry. 'He usually drops in at lunchtime.'

'I'd prefer it if you did it. I'll be busy then.'

Barry looked at her oddly. She wondered if he suspected something but he said nothing. 'I'll tell him. But I bet he wants to talk to you.'

She hadn't seen Mike since their meeting in the Drovers' Arms. In time she knew she'd have to speak to him—he was her mother's surgeon after all. But for the moment she'd rather keep her distance from him. He disturbed her.

At lunchtime, when apparently Mike usually called, she intended to stay in her room. There was always paperwork to catch up on. But one of the trainee nurses knocked and put her head round the door. 'Angel, there's that Mr Gilmour come in to see Suzanne. I was just going to feed her and he wants to know if it'll be all right if he does it?'

Angel thought. After her shaky start Suzanne had been gaining strength daily. There was now no need to feed her through a nasogastric tube, she could be held and fed her tiny amount of milk by hand. Often Angel did it herself. She knew was getting very attached to the infant.

'I don't see any reason why not,' she said. 'But you stay in the room and if you're worried about anything at all, tell him.'

This trainee still thought that all doctors were wonderful. 'I couldn't tell a surgeon what to do!' she gasped.

'Mr Gilmour wouldn't mind at all,' Angel said with certainty. 'But if you like, I'll tell him.' It struck her that this might be the best way to re-establish their essentially professional relationship.

He was standing, as he so often was, looking down in the incubator. As ever, there was no way of telling what he was thinking from his expression. Then Angel noticed what he was wearing, and she sighed gently. A dark suit, a white shirt, a black tie. Dress suitable for a funeral.

'You want to feed Suzanne yourself?' she asked him.

He nodded. 'I've noticed that the other...the parents are shown how to do it. I thought I should learn how myself.'

'We encourage the parents to do it as soon as it's safe. Ideally, babies should have instant physical contact with their mothers, it promotes bonding. But if they're in an incubator, it's hard.'

'I do know the theory, Sister, and I agree with it.' There was just a touch of dry humour in his voice.

'I'll get her out, then, and we'll prepare her feed. Sit there and let me put a towel on your lap.'

When he was sitting she waved to the nurse to fetch the milk, opened the incubator and took Suzanne out. There was that indefinable—to her, exciting—baby smell. She wrapped Suzanne, offered her to his gentle hands. Then the feed arrived.

'Nurse Fawkes here will stay with you,' Angel said formally. 'If there's any problem or question at all, please, ask her.'

'Of course,' he said equally formally.

'I'll be in my room if you need to speak to me.'

As she left she looked back through the glass door of the incubator room. He had forgotten her, and was staring down at Suzanne. There was something infinitely caring about the curve of his head and neck, the way his arm held the little bundle. Angel felt tears prickle in the corners of her eyes.

Twenty minutes later he did call at her room, where she had a coffee waiting for him. 'You've been to a funeral?' she asked directly.

'My sister's funeral. Suzanne's mother, Monica. I was the only mourner, Angel, and I felt sad that anyone could be buried with not a single person there who really cared for them.'

She could feel his desolation. 'I'm so sorry, Mike. We've had our differences, but I would have come with you if I'd known. I've got very fond of Suzanne and, as you say, this was her mother.'

'Well, thanks for the thought anyway. Eric Whitby conducted the service. He was...he was helpful. He couldn't have taken more care if the chapel had been full, instead of just the two of us. He talked about learning from the past and looking forward to the future. The funeral was the end of something but now I've got to think of Suzanne.'

'Does Eric know about your past?' Angel was anxious.

Mike smiled briefly. 'I didn't tell him we were married. I did tell him about the way Monica and I were brought up. But now, how is Suzanne?'

Angel relaxed. His tone was friendly, their argument at the Drovers' Arms apparently forgotten. Well, this was what she wanted, a proper relationship between carer and guardian. 'We're all very pleased with her progress.

She had a shaky start but now she's doing fine. Are you making arrangements about what to do when she's discharged?'

'I'm thinking about it, but it's a nightmare. Some solution will come to me—it'll have to. There are two problems really. First, I've got to find someone to look after her here in Micklethwaite, just for the next few months. I thought of asking you if you could recommend anyone, Angel. You seem to know everyone round here.'

'I'll have a think. What's the second problem?'

'The bigger problem is when I go down to London. For the first year or so I'll be working like a lunatic. The job needs—deserves—someone who can give it all their attention. But I couldn't give it that attention unless I was certain that Suzanne was happy. I'll have to find a nanny, or a set of nurses to take over. Money's not the problem, getting the right people is.'

'I wondered,' she said. 'I'm afraid I wondered...when she was first born and I knew about your plans for the future...I wondered if you'd want to keep her.'

He shrugged. 'I'll be honest, Angel—just for a while so did I. But then I stood there and looked at her and knew I had no choice. I wanted her.'

For a moment they were both silent.

She didn't quite know why she said it. 'I told you before—I've got very fond of Suzanne, Mike. If you just can't work something out—and if you can get someone to help—I'll look after her for a while. If you need me.' Then she sat back, appalled at what she had just said.

'D'you mean that? Please, Angel, just think about what you've said. It was something you said quickly, you haven't had time to think about all of what it might entail. I'll quite understand if you realise it's quite impractical.'

She frowned. 'It was just meant as a last resort, if everything else didn't go well for you—for Suzanne, that is. It's her I'm thinking of. I've still got my mother to worry about first and, of course, we're still trying to move. Make what plans you can, Mike, and if eventually you're really desperate I'll see what can be done, depending on my situation.'

'That's very good of you, it's an offer I really appreciate. But you know, Angel, it doesn't surprise me that it comes from you.' He lifted his cup, looked at it in surprise. 'Empty? Any chance of another cupful? You always made wonderful coffee.'

She poured him one, mildly pleased by his compliment, and spoke without thinking. 'When we had a morning off together you always got up first and made us tea in bed. Then I would get up...later...and make us coffee.'

'Later?' he said without inflection, and she blushed.

For quite a while neither of them spoke. Then he said neutrally, 'You're not your usual self Angel. Your voice is a bit flat and you look...well, defeated. I won't flatter myself that I'm the cause. Not had any bad news, have you?'

She had never been able to conceal anything from him. At times his ability to recognise her moods had been almost upsetting. There were some things she needed to keep to herself but, she supposed, this wasn't one of them.

'The bungalow you looked around—the one we were trying to buy. The agents have written to me. Someone has offered an extra three thousand pounds. There's no way I can find that, I'm stretching my limit already.'

'But won't selling High Walls bring in some money?'

She shook her head. 'Not much, because we can't sell it. It's held in trust for the family—perhaps in time my brother's children or even my children might farm it. But for the moment we've agreed to lease the building to a neighbour—Mr Martlett of Brock Farm. He already leases the land.'

'So you can't buy the bungalow?'

'Not unless I can find three thousand pounds in the next three days. That's all the time the agent can allow us.'

'A pity. That bungalow would have suited your mother perfectly. Angel, let me emphasise, High Walls isn't good for your mother.'

'I know that! But I can't find somewhere suitable and she won't move. She's stubborn.'

'It seems to be a family trait. Sorry, Angel, didn't mean to be personal. I really took to your mother.'

Three days later she saw that the bungalow had a SOLD sign outside. Well, she had expected it. But it still felt hard, and she was rather depressed when she walked into the ward.

Mike came in at lunchtime as he nearly always did, and asked to have a word. 'Angel, we need to have another talk somewhere out of the hospital. Could we go to the Drovers' Arms again?'

'Why? I thought things were going well between us. And the last time we talked there we had a fight. I just don't see the point.'

'There is a point,' he said patiently, 'but standing up in the middle of a busy neonatal ward isn't the place to consider it.'

'Is it about Suzanne?'

'Partly, but there's something else a bit more important. Listen, we really do need to talk.'

Angel sighed. 'All right, then, we could go when I finish this shift—if you can get away. Ma is expecting me, but I'll phone and tell her I'll be late.'

She wasn't really sure how she felt about this. Once she had accepted, she felt almost pleased at the prospect of a drink with him. That wasn't good.

She didn't like the way her mother coughed when she phoned but knew it would be no use telling her to go to bed. Some things never changed.

Mike was waiting for her at the same place in the entrance to the Drovers' Arms. He fetched her a fruit juice as before and insisted that she have a sandwich as well.

'I want you comfortable and relaxed,' he said, 'and I want you to promise me that you won't lose your temper. You'll listen to everything I have to say before saying anything.'

She bit into her sandwich. 'That is a bad way to start the conversation. I'm curious, of course—but I'm angry already. You've got something in mind for me, and you think I won't like it. Mike, we're not married any more. You have no say in my life and I owe you nothing.'

'Are you going to listen to everything I have to say?'

'Oh, yes. I'll listen. As I said, I'm curious.'

Now he didn't seem to know where to start. 'You told me there was no chance of you buying the bungalow that you wanted?'

'That's true. And it's gone now, I saw the sold sign this morning. Someone could offer three thousand more than I had.'

'It didn't go for three thousand more. Someone else offered five thousand, in cash, on condition that they could move in immediately.'

'Good luck to them,' she muttered. 'It must be nice to have all the money you need. How did you know that, Mike?'

'Well, I was curious.' He drummed his fingers on the table a moment, looked thoughtful. 'Just for a minute I want to go back to when we got divorced. The agreement you sent out to me stated that in our settlement you made no claims on my estate, or on my present or future income.'

'I didn't want anything from you,' she said. 'I could earn my own living.'

'But you knew I was earning a vast salary in the States. When I showed the agreement to a lawyer myself he was astounded, said I was the luckiest divorced man he'd ever met. I'd even been sending you money while we were still married and you'd saved it and sent it all back.'

'I had my pride,' she said.

'How well I know that! Well, Angel, for all your pride, I felt beholden to you. Now it's only fair that you should be beholden to me.'

She was lost, she just couldn't see the point of this conversation. 'What are you talking about?'

He took a mouthful of his beer and then said, 'I bought the bungalow.'

It took a moment for what he had said to sink in. 'You did what?'

'I bought the bungalow. I have plenty of cash. I've saved most of what I was paid in America.'

'We showed you round that bungalow, Mike! You'd never heard of it till my mother told you about it. Mike, this is truly despicable! I never thought you'd stoop to anything like this. You look round the place as our guest, then creep off to the estate agent and—'

'Angel, I didn't! There was absolutely no chance of you buying the place, you said so yourself. Didn't you? Well?'

It hurt, but she had to admit he was right. 'I suppose so. Yes, I did. There was no way I could afford an extra three thousand pounds.

But why do you want it? It's no good to you. You're going off to London in a few months, it's not worthwhile moving into a place for that short time. I hope you're not going to keep it as a holiday cottage!'

'Very true, it's not worth my while moving in and, no, I'm not going to use it as a holiday cottage. Now, Angel, take a deep breath, have a drink and try to listen without losing your temper! This is serious. It concerns you and your mother.'

Perfectly calmly, she said, 'Please, say what you have to, and then I can get home.'

'Right. I have a proposal for you and your mother.' He paused, took a deep breath himself. 'I have bought Valley View. Think of it as an investment if you like. I would like to offer you a long lease on the property, you can move in at once. I've got a few calculations here, this is what I think is a fair return for me.' He pushed a piece of paper across the table to her.

She looked at what he had written, then pushed the paper back. 'Mike, you know very well that that rent is far too low. My mother and I don't want charity!'

'I knew I could rely on you to get angry,' he muttered. 'Angel, can't you just take it that this is something I want to do?'

'Why should you want to be so generous to my mother and me?'

'Well, for a start, I want to help your mother. And though this might be a lot of money to you—I don't want to boast, but it isn't a lot to me.'

'There's more to it than that, Mike. This is a very generous gesture on your part. Why?'

He didn't seem to want to answer. He drank some beer, rubbed his face, gazed vaguely round the room. Then he seemed to make up his mind about something. Looking at her intently, he said, 'We were married for nine months and I was happy then. I still have some…regard for you. I am in a position to help. I'd like to because I know perfectly well that if the situation were the other way about, you would do the same for me. Wouldn't you?'

The last two words were a challenge, and she knew she had to answer honestly. She couldn't take her eyes from his face as she desperately wondered what she could tell him.

But eventually she said, 'Yes, I would do the same for you. And I still have some—we'll call it regard for you. But Mike, make no mistake, it isn't love. That has gone.'

'Are you sure?'

'I'm absolutely certain.' She didn't want to talk about this, she felt she had given away too much already. 'Now, let's get back on the subject. What else are you getting out of this?'

'Nothing. This would be a purely business arrangement between your mother and you and me. If you're interested, perhaps you would get your solicitor to write to me.'

'I'll have to talk it over with Ma, but I know she'll be delighted.' Angel thought for a minute, reviewed the conversation she'd just had. There was something she had left out. 'Mike,' she said, trying not to sound grudging, 'this is a very generous offer on your part, and you know we're going to accept. From my mother and myself—thank you very much.'

He grinned. 'There,' he said, 'that didn't hurt very much, did it?'

For a moment she looked at him in horror—but then she had to laugh. 'Mike Gilmour, you know me too well.'

'I'll fetch us another drink,' he said.

It was good to have a short break from the conversation, she was more relaxed when he returned. 'Have you got anywhere in deciding on Suzanne's future?' she asked.

'Possibly I have, there's been an offer. Sister Parkin works on one of my wards and I—'

Angel stood, leaned over the table. 'You let Grace Parkin anywhere near Suzanne and I'll phone Social Services and see that the child is adopted! Grace is selfish, mercenary, idle and a disgrace to the nursing profession. I'm shocked that you could even—'

He laughed. 'I know all that. Give me credit for some sense, Angel. Sister Parkin made me an offer, I asked a couple of questions and then refused it. I just mentioned her to show you how hard it is to get someone exactly right. But I'm still looking. Now, sit down and finish your drink.'

'Don't do anything like that to me again,' she said, 'even as a joke.' Then she took a card from her bag and slid it across to him. 'That's the name and address of someone I will recommend to you,' she said. 'Her name is Nancy Timms. She was a children's nurse for years and she'd be delighted to help you with Suzanne. She lives only a hundred yards from High Walls.'

'Is that significant?' Mike asked quietly.

She hesitated, then said, 'As you know, I've got very fond of Suzanne. If I had the chance to take her out in the pram every now and again. I'd like that. But my recommendation has nothing to do with that.'

'I know you only want to best for your goddaughter. And I'll phone this Nancy Timms tonight.'

It was three days later when he phoned.

'Hi Angel,' he said. 'I've been to have a long talk with Nancy Timms. I've asked about her around the hospital and I think she's wonderful. However, a problem has come up since she agreed to take Suzanne in. Her daughter has got to go into hospital and Nancy will be going over to her son-in-law's to help with the children on occasion. She's willing to look after Suzanne whenever needed but, of course, is not always going to be at home.'

'So now you need somewhere for her to stay in the meantime?' she asked after a pause.

'Yes. I certainly can't take her to live with me in the residency.'

She decided to take the plunge. 'Mike, you did us a great kindness in offering us Valley View. But if you need the place for yourself and Suzanne...'

'No Angel—it's for you and your mother. I wouldn't dream of backing out of our arrangement now.'

'Thank you Mike. In that case, we may be able to help you in return. Nancy actually told me about her daughter yesterday morning and my mother and I have had a long talk. This isn't a sudden thing, we've talked it through and slept on it and talked it through again. If it all can be arranged—if we can agree—we'd like to offer Suzanne a home while you're in Micklekirk and just till you're fully settled in London and have found a nurse or something. Sort of share her with Nancy so one of us will always be available. I've got...very close to Suzanne and would love to take care of her as well.'

There was no immediate reply and the silence between them seemed to stretch on into infinity. 'Mike...are you there?' she asked eventually.

'I'm here. I'm just too— You say you've talked this over with your mother? And you're absolutely certain yourself?'

'I said that to start with,' she pointed out, 'and you know I don't say what I don't mean.'

'Yes, I know that. My first reaction is to say that I can't think of anything better. But...your mother isn't well and I'm not sure a baby in the house is the best thing for her. At least, not till well after her operation. I need time to think, Angel. Shall we have another session in the Drovers'? Say tomorrow night?'

'We're becoming regulars,' she muttered. 'All right, I'll see you there at eight.'

They now had their favourite table at the Drovers' and the barman recognised them and smiled. Mike bought their drinks and they faced each other, each obviously uneasy. 'I've thought about this quite a bit,' he said. 'Here's a proposal, but we can negotiate if there's anything you don't like. This is only a rough plan.'

'I'm listening,' she said.

'Right. Both you and Nancy would need to co-ordinate Suzanne's living arrangements and care. I can help out, too, when I'm available, but you would ultimately be sharing the bulk of the work between you. You mother's operation is due and she will need to recuperate—we must take her health into account and make sure we don't cause her any stress before or after.'

'Nancy will keep an eye on her while I'm not there and if it becomes necessary, Ma is happy to stay at my brother's for a while. We can do this Mike,' she said firmly. 'She'll be cared for as well as Suzanne will be, don't you worry, and she'll soon be back on her feet again.'

He smiled. 'That's good to hear. In return for all your help, for the time you have her, I want you to have the bungalow rent free. When I come to leave Micklekirk I'll take Suzanne off your hands. I'm going to search desperately for someone to help me look after her in London.'

'You don't want to be parted from her, do you?' Angel asked with some interest.

'No I don't. When she came into my life first I was...confused, but now things are different. I want her with me always. We nearly had a child Angel and I—'

'We're not talking about that now! This meeting is about Suzanne.'

'Yes. Of course. It would be easier for Nancy and her family if Suzanne could stay some of the time in Valley View.'

'We can work well with Nancy,' said Angel. 'We've already talked to her about it.'

'Good. The next thing is, I want a complete set of everything a new baby needs. You can get me a list, can't you?'

She was overwhelmed. 'Yes, I can get you a list. But, Mike, you don't have to—'

'Not only do I have to, I want to. And do you know any good local workmen?'

'I know everyone round here,' she said, her shoulders slumping. 'Anything you need doing I can get done.'

It seemed as if she was being dragged more and more into Mike's life again. And, what was worse, she was quite enjoying it.

CHAPTER FOUR

IT HAPPENED at nine o'clock at night, three days later. Angel had eaten the tea Marion had cooked, they had chatted for a while and then her mother had wrapped herself in a shawl and gone to watch television in the chilly sitting room.

Angel sat at the kitchen table to run through her lists of jobs to be done and things to be bought. She hadn't quite realised what a lot of stuff needed to be bought when a newborn was coming into the household. And in the past she had advised new mums what they needed! This was learning at the sharp end. But...it was fun.

Mike had been typically direct about this. 'I want to buy what is needed. I don't want you trying to economise, trying to save me money. Whatever is necessary we'll get. I have every faith in your judgement.'

'I know someone with a second-hand pram that—'

'No. A new pram. Perhaps I'm being foolish, but you can give in to my whims.'

So a new pram was on the list—with cot, bath, baby clothes, no end of things. She was taking a guilty pleasure in making the list. Shopping would be fun.

At five to nine she decided to make herself a cup of tea, called through to the living room to ask her mother if she would like one, too. No reply. Probably dozing, Angel thought with a smile, and went to ask in person.

Her mother was slumped on one end of the couch, her face white, her breathing laboured. 'Ma! What happened!'

She could just make out the answer. 'Worst pain yet. Don't think I can move. Help me…help me up, Angelina.'

Angel was a nurse as well as a daughter. There was no time for emotion now, she had work to do. Quickly she pulled her mother upright, after which she could breathe more easily. After a while her mother looked slightly better.

'I'm going to phone an ambulance, Ma. You should be in hospital.'

'No! I'm all right, it was just a twinge. You know I've had them before. Now I've had my tablets I'll be all right.'

'You've never had one as bad as this and I think you ought to— Not now!'

The phone was ringing. Why did the phone always ring when it was completely the wrong time? 'Answer it,' her mother commanded. 'I can't stand the sound of a ringing phone.'

So Angel answered it. 'Yes!' she snapped.

'Not the most welcoming greeting I've ever heard,' a calm voice said. 'It's Mike, Angel. If this isn't a convenient time I can ring back later.'

'Mike? I'm sorry, I didn't mean anything. I'm a bit, well, I think—that is, I know my mother's just had another heart attack and she refuses to let me ring for an ambulance…'

'Does she need an ambulance? D'you want me to send one?' His voice was harsh, efficient now.

'I don't really think so. I was scared, Mike. I thought she might have… She's had these before, but never quite as bad as this.'

'Keep her warm, keep her upright. If her condition gets even slightly worse, send for the ambulance and ignore what she says. I'll be there in twenty minutes.'

'But, Mike, there's no need...' Too late. The buzzing noise told her that he had already rung off.

He arrived in less than twenty minutes and she shuddered to think how he must have driven. It usually took her over half an hour. He was dressed in jeans and sweater, which contrasted with the doctor's bag.

'It's so good of you to come, Mike, but I could have sent for the GP or an ambulance. But I'm glad you're here.'

He followed her as she led him into the sitting room where her mother was sitting, now bundled in a couple of blankets. 'In a sense she's my patient already,' he pointed out. 'I've got her on my list for an operation. Call this pre-op preparation. Hello, Marion. You look just a touch under the weather.'

'Round here the weather's always bad,' she said, perhaps misunderstanding him.

'It certainly is. Now, tell me exactly what happened, and how you felt.' After she told him he gave her a quick examination, then stood there, frowning. 'Marion, I don't want any argument, it won't do you any good. I'm admitting you to hospital. I'll phone and arrange a bed while Angel packs you a case. There's no real need for an ambulance, so I'll take you in my car and your daughter can follow in hers.'

'Am I really so bad that I need to go to hospital?'

'If you stay here and have another of those attacks then you'll know what being really bad means.' He turned to Angel. 'Can we leave as quickly as possible? I'd like to get her under proper observation.'

'Of course,' said Angel.

They drove in convoy down to the hospital, Mike obviously driving so as to shake Marion as little as possible. There was a bed waiting in the cardiac ward. Angel said hello to the nurse whom she knew, and then to the house officer who would book her mother in. She gave what details were necessary and then sat in the little waiting room. She knew better than to interfere with other people's work.

After ten minutes Mike rejoined her. 'How d'you feel?' he asked.

'Well, you whipping her into hospital has made me feel worse,' she said. 'I didn't think she was this bad.'

'Possibly not, but it's as well to be careful. One thing, though, Angel. I'm not discharging her back into that freezing house.'

'I know you're right,' she said dismally. 'I'll sort something out. It's a shame the bungalow isn't ready yet.' Then she smiled. 'Ma is very much looking forward to moving into Valley View and seeing more of Suzanne. She misses children. She'll be so happy to take charge when she's well enough. And I know Suzanne will be a lovely child to look after.'

'You do?' There was humour in his voice. 'You can tell how a premature baby will develop, even though you've only nursed her for a short while?'

'Yes, I can,' she told him seriously. 'Cardiac surgeons aren't expert in everything, you know. When you've nursed prems as long as I have, you get to know how they'll behave, how they'll develop. Babies are as different as people, Mike.'

'So you think you can tell her character already?'

'I certainly do. Suzanne is a fighter. Remember that night when we had her bap tised?'

'I remember it,' he said shortly. 'Not a night I want to recall.'

'Quite. Well, take it from me, a lot of babies would have given up, they would have died. She didn't. And that's how she'll be all her life.'

'I like listening to you talk about babies,' he said. 'You're enthusiastic, you love them. It's a side of you that was there but I never appreciated before—'

She thought about that. 'I think I've been complimented,' she said, 'but I'm not really sure.'

'You've been visiting your mother so you know she's a lot better,' Mike said five days later. 'She could be discharged tomorrow, but the question is, discharged to where? We've agreed not High Walls. And I don't think she's ready to move into the bungalow yet. And the bungalow certainly isn't ready for her.'

'It's all been arranged,' said Angel. 'I mentioned my brother Martin to you. He lives in

London, and married with two children. Ma can go to live with them for three weeks. She dotes on the kids and she gets on very well with Alice, Martin's wife. They wanted her to live with them, but she said there was no way she'd live in suburbia.'

'Marion does have definite views about some things,' he agreed. 'Martin knows how your mother is?'

'Of course! I rang him the night Ma had her attack and I've rung every day since. He's a very busy man but he wanted to fly up at once. I told him there was no need.'

'So you're a close family? You never talked about your brother before.'

She frowned. 'That time…those months we were married…somehow they seemed a different part of my life. They weren't connected to where I'd been brought up, or the friends and family I had. In time we would all have met and got on together. But it didn't happen.'

'No, it didn't happen.' They were sitting in his room at the hospital, the cubbyhole with nothing but a desk and three chairs, a computer terminal and shelves full of books and files. He rolled a pencil across the desk, they both listened to the tiny rattle. 'Do you think…because I was a different part of your life, it was easier to cut me out?'

A few weeks ago she would have snarled at Mike that her reasons for leaving him were her own business. But he had asked gently, and it was a reasonable question.

'Probably,' she said. 'When you'd gone there was a big emptiness. But I didn't have to explain to anyone, didn't have to endure people's pity or compassion or even annoyance. Since they didn't know about you they didn't miss you. And that made it easier. How did you feel in America?'

She was wary about this conversation. Somehow they had strayed from talking about her mother, which was safe, to talking about themselves. And that usually led to a fight. But so far they had managed to remain calm. And she genuinely wanted to know how he had felt.

'I had no friends out there, only colleagues. People were only interested in my work, not in me. So I guess I was able to compartmentalise you. You were a thing apart. And I worked till I dropped and when I dropped I slept.'

'I did something similar. I gave up the Buxton job, went to South America. That was hard work, too.'

'Our parting seems distant now. As if it happened to someone else.'

She thought. That was exactly right. She *could* look back on it as if it had happened to someone else. 'Perhaps it was my fault in the beginning,' she said. 'I got that really good nursing job in Buxton. I hadn't really liked living in Manchester, but because I was with you I'd managed to tolerate it. And that tolerance disappeared. Buxton was so close to the countryside I felt I could breathe again. When you didn't have to live in the hospital you stayed with me and commuted into work. Lots of people did. You could have carried on doing it.'

'But, instead, three months later I was offered a wonder job in Boston. We flew out there together to look round. I thought we could make it work.'

Now she knew her voice was getting louder, she even sounded shrill. 'I hated it. I knew it was a brilliant career move for you, but I would have been actively miserable living there. So we decided you would go on your own.'

'Did we make the right decision, Angel?'

'You would have been foolish to turn it down. It was a young doctor's dream job. But since we were going to be apart indefinitely and things weren't right between us, I decided we might as well get divorced. And now we've both been successful in our own ways and we've managed well without each other.'

'Apparently,' he said. 'Have you been happy?'

That was an unfair question. 'Well, happyish. As much as anyone is, I guess. I enjoy my work, my friends, the countryside.'

'Was there no other reason for you wanting a divorce? I mean, apart from us being so much apart? You said things weren't right between us.'

'There was the baby. Look, Mike, can we talk about something else?'

She felt uneasy. This conversation was getting too intimate, she didn't want to know how Mike had felt, or him to know how she had felt. It was important to keep their distance. Only that way could they work together.

'Anyway,' she said in a brighter voice, 'Ma will go down to stay with Martin for a few weeks. He'll fly up, stay the night with me and fly her back the next day. There's a very good air service between the coast and London.'

'Yes, I know. I use it quite often.' Now he was being practical, professional. 'When will it be convenient for your brother to fetch your mother?'

'I'll phone him at his office this lunchtime and then let you know.'

Martin was a busy businessman but he had his priorities right. He told Angel that he would fly up the next day, he was looking forward to a night at High Walls. 'Bring your fleece-lined pyjamas,' she told him. This isn't the soft, centrally heated South.'

'I know that, little sister. Remember, I grew up there, too. Now, what's the name of this surgeon again?'

She was needed for something on the ward then, so it was half an hour before she had time to phone Mike.

His voice sounded amused, as it so often did. 'I've already heard from brother Martin,' he said. 'He wants a meeting.'

'What? The three of us?'

'No. He specifically asked just to talk to me. Man talk, I suppose.'

'Mike, that's not funny! You talk to Martin about my mother, not about me. And you are, above all, not to tell him that we were married!'

'I wouldn't do that, Angel, unless you wanted me to. No, I think that Martin wants to talk about the arrangement that is to exist between you, your mother and me. And I think that is a good thing. I'd like your interests to be well represented.'

'I can look after myself,' she mumbled.

Martin refused to be met by her at the airport. He would have a hired car waiting, as it would be much simpler. 'Not sure I trust that banger of yours, Angel. I'll come straight to the hospital, see you and this Mr Gilmour then visit Ma. Next morning I'll take her home. The kids are really looking forward to her coming.'

'It'll be good to see you, Martin, even if it is a flying visit.' She was still not sure about Martin and Mike being together without her. In spite of Mike's assurances, she wondered what they would talk about.

But everything seemed to go well. Martin arrived, looked round her ward, went to see Mike, visited his mother. In the evening he toured the bungalow then took Angel to dinner in the Cat and Fiddle. 'I like the bungalow and I like Mike Gilmour,' he said. 'We talked about the bungalow and you looking after the baby for a while, and I think it's fine. He's getting a lot, of course—I know what bringing up a child takes—but he's letting you virtually have the bungalow and has ensured Ma's future and well-being. Strange he's not married. Don't fancy him, do you, little sister?'

'No!' She knew the answer came out too curt, too definite.

'Pity.' He took a deep draught of his beer. 'I still think there's something you're not telling me, little sister, but I know you will in time. Now, since we can walk home from here, I'll have another pint of this excellent bitter.'

She liked being with her brother, they had once been very close and it was a pity he lived so far away. But she had forgotten how shrewd he could be.

Next morning she went to the cardiac ward with Martin and together they took her mother down to his car. To her surprise, Mike had come into the ward, too.

'I'm only going for a few weeks,' Marion had said. 'It'll be lovely to see my grandchildren, but I've got work to do when I get back.'

'There's an operation you've got to have,' Mike had replied, 'then more recuperation and then you can start work. But don't worry, I've got a vested interest in seeing you up and fit.'

Mike and Angel waved goodbye as the car pulled off. 'Years of work in her,' said Mike, 'after she's had the operation.'

'Don't worry,' said Angel, 'we'll both stick to our half of the bargain.'

It was amazing how fast things could be done when people were willing to push. Mike got access to the bungalow practically at once. Her solicitor drew up an agreement between them, with a great deal of frowning and nose-pinching. He had been the family solicitor for years.

'One thing I must make clear,' he told her, 'this agreement gives you no rights of access to the child after she leaves you. I know it will be only for a few months—but whatever relationship you may have formed will then be entirely at the mercy of Mr Gilmour. Are you willing to accept that?'

'I'm a professional nurse, I know the dangers of getting too attached to my patients.'

'This is something entirely different,' he told her.

The agreement with Mr Martlett was equally speedy. He would take over High Walls at once, he had plans to turn it into a hostel for walkers. One of the outbuildings would remain in their name. They could store furniture and so on in it and there was easy access to it.

She kept away from Mike as much as possible. The last couple of times they had met she had been too relaxed in his company, she needed to keep him at a distance. When he came to the ward to see Suzanne, she stayed in her room.

But eventually they had to meet as there was much to be decided. She had already been making lists of what they needed to buy and they needed to check them together. There were also legal matters to be considered. Eventually Social Services would be involved.

Mike phoned the ward with an invitation one morning. 'So far we've had drinks and snacks at the Drovers' Arms,' he said. 'Let's see how what their dinners are like.'

She didn't really want to have dinner with him. It would be too friendly, too intimate. 'I'm afraid I'm very busy at High Walls. I've got things to do there. I don't really have the time for dinner.'

There were problems on the ward. In the middle of the night they had admitted baby Ellen, a full-term child who had been born with an exomphalos—a hernia—and some of her intestines protruded through her umbilicus. Fortunately the protrusion wasn't too large. A damp sterile dressing was draped over it and baby Ellen put in an incubator.

Because her intestines were blocked she couldn't be fed by mouth. She took nourishment from a dextrose drip and she screamed constantly.

Baby Ellen would need an operation, quite a minor one but requiring a specialist surgeon. Only the very largest hospitals had specialist paediatric surgeons, so the baby would have to be transferred. The consultant phoned and arranged the transfer.

'Angel, if it's possible, I'd like you to accompany the baby,' Linda said.

Angel checked her staffing rota, and decided it was possible. No matter how well trained the ambulance paramedics might be, the baby had to be accompanied by her own nurse.

There was a special portable incubator for the journey, with a syringe drip fitted. The baby was moved into the portable incubator and Angel checked that all was well—that the monitor was functioning, the oxygen supply ready.

She introduced herself to the two paramedics, Joe and Marge, and soon they were on their fifty-mile journey to the coast.

It was a typical moors day, overcast and cold to start with and then with heavy rain beating against the ambulance. But it was warm inside. Angel chatted casually to the paramedics and kept a wary eye on Ellen. But there was no trouble.

They were expected. The baby was transferred efficiently, they had a quick cup of coffee and set off back. She would be back in plenty of time for her date with Mike. No, it wasn't a date. It was a meeting.

It happened, as it so often did, at the worst time and the worst place. The wind and rain had increased, buffeting the ambulance as it wound across one of the least hospitable sections of land for miles. This was high country, with only a rare farmhouse to relieve the bleakness of moor and sky.

The radio crackled, she half listened to the paramedics' quiet conversation. Then Marge looked into the back where she was sitting on the stretcher.

'Got a problem, Angel. There's a 999 call been made from one of these farms. We're by far the nearest and we've got to respond.'

'No problem,' said Angel. She knew that ambulances had to answer 999 calls, no matter what else they were doing. They would have answered the call even if they had been carrying the baby and incubator. 'What's the emergency?'

Marge laughed. 'You're going to like this because you might get involved. It's a birth. A real chapter of incidents. First, the midwife was driving out but she got high on the moors and then skidded off the road into a ditch. Her mobile phone wasn't charged so it took her half an hour to walk to where she could phone in for help. And the husband has no idea what to do and he's panicking. Meanwhile, even though it's a first baby, it turns out that this is going to be one of those super-rapid births. Contractions only four minutes apart.'

'Four minutes apart! D'you think we'll get there before the baby?'

'We're certainly going to try.' At that moment the ambulance turned off the road, bumped and slid along a muddy drive towards a grey stone building sheltering under the side of a hill. There was no other building within sight. 'No neighbours to run to for help,' said Marge. 'This is a great set-up for a first baby.'

Angel didn't know what the etiquette was for these occasions. She had a vast respect for ambulance paramedics, who sometimes had to deal with the most horrendous of accidents. 'Look,' she said, 'I know you're trained for this and you've probably helped with dozens of births. But I'm also a trained midwife, and if you want me to help I will.'

'Don't want you to help,' grunted Joe. 'We want you to do it. Don't we, Marge?'

'Our own portable midwife? Too true, we want her to do it.'

After a while they skidded to a halt in the farmyard, outside the front door. Marge and Joe grabbed a bag each, ran through the rain to the shelter of the porch. Angel followed them. As they ran the door opened. A man waved to them frantically.

All three ran into the front room. 'She's in there,' the farmer cried, and pointed to another door. They could all hear a woman crying in pain.

Joe and Marge held back. Angel looked at the frightened face of the young girl on the bed and said, 'Hi, I'm Sister Angel Thwaite and I'm here to help. Don't worry, everything's going to be all right now. What's your name?'

'Jenny, Jenny Armstrong. I—Ooh!'

Angel pulled back the covers, placed her hand on Jenny's abdomen. It was obvious the waters had broken. Automatically she timed the interval between contractions. Three minutes—not a lot of time to waste. She turned and said, 'There's no way we can load Jenny into the ambulance now, this baby's going to be born right here.'

Baseline observations first. Using the kit that Marge provided, Angel took the temperature, blood pressure, pulse and respiration rate. She scribbled the results on a handy bit of paper. Then she listened to the baby with a Pinard's stethescope and conducted an internal examination. Head was at plus two.

To one side of Jenny's bed was a cot, and nearby was the pack that the midwife had obviously left. Angel tore it open, slipped on a pair of gloves. 'Do you want to take the baby?' she asked Marge. 'I think we'll have the action in a couple of minutes.'

To Jenny she said gently, 'would you like your husband to come in?'

'Yes, yes, please. I want him here.' With a grim attempt at a smile she gasped, 'He can see what it's really like.'

After that it was straightforward.

The baby boy had been born and was on his mother's breast when the midwife arrived, wet from her earlier walk but determined. She had been driven by the proprietor of a local garage.

Once she was satisfied that all was well, the farmer found her something to change into. Then Angel handed over to her officially, signed the Apgar form and left her name and hospital address. Then she climbed back into the ambulance. 'Going to be no end of paperwork to sort this out,' Joe said gleefully.

When she had a moment Angel used her own mobile phone to ring Mike to explain that she would be late. He understood at once. 'Glad for the girl that you were there. D'you want to cancel our meeting, then?'

'I'd rather not. Can I phone you when I'm nearly back? We could still meet no matter how late it is.'

'That's good. Don't worry, I appreciate what you have to do. But phone me no matter how late you are.' He rang off.

She rang Mike when they were near the hospital. It was nine-thirty and she was exhausted, but she still wanted to meet him. Things had to be sorted out.

'How long since you ate?' he asked as soon as they were sitting in the Drovers' Arms.

How long since she'd eaten? She couldn't remember. It had been too much of a day, she'd been too busy to eat. 'Well, I had a sandwich at lunchtime. But, really Mike, I'm fine, I don't need anything—'

'You look terrible, your blood sugar level must be down in your boots. For once, don't argue, I'll get what you need.'

With his pint of beer he fetched her a brandy, and shortly afterwards there was a hot pie for her, brown-crusted and smelling wonderful, with great golden chips and salad on the side. 'You need calories and some comfort eating,' he said. 'Finish that and you'll feel better. Mind if I steal a chip?'

So she ate, and when she had finished she felt much better. 'That was good,' she said. 'I feel that I can face the world now. And whatever you propose, I'll agree to. The way to a woman's heart is through her stomach.'

'I know that. One of the good things I do remember about you is that you enjoyed eating. No lettuce-leaf diets when you'd put on half an ounce.'

'Hey, we're here to work, not trip down memory lane.'

'Very true. In fact, there's so much to remember that I've got a little notebook.' He produced it with great pride. 'I write down jobs on one side of the paper, and tick them off on the other side when they're done.'

'And then write down new things to do?'

'You've spotted the weakness in the system. And I can even envisage having to buy a new notebook. Now...surveyors' report. I told him I wanted the place fixed so that nothing would need doing once you were in. This is what he suggested.'

She peered in the book and flinched. 'Rather a lot there.'

'I want there to be no problems later. And I want it painted inside and out.'

'But I was going to decorate the inside! I'm good at it.'

'Don't I know it. Top flat, 2 Grove Street—it took you two weekends to turn that place into a little palace. I loved living there.'

The flat at 2 Grove Street. She hadn't thought about it in years. Yes, it had been a little palace and she had... 'That was then,' she said. 'Circumstances have changed now.'

'Of course. But you've got better things to do than shin up ladders. We'll get a contractor to come in. May I leave the choice of colours and so on to you?'

She felt a stirring of interest, this was going to be fun. 'If you like. Do you want to pick the colours for your room, though?'

'No, I want to leave everything to you. Now, can you recommend any good firms? I know no one around here.'

'There's a firm of contractors in the village that I know well,' she said. 'They'll do anything—gas fitting, plumbing, electrical work, painting and so on, too. They might not be the cheapest firm but they'll be the best.'

'Just what we need. Now, you were making me a list of baby things needed? I told you I didn't want a secondhand pram.'

'I remember.' She passed over a piece of paper. 'This is the list I used to hand out to soon-to-be mums. Some of the things are more important than others and—'

'We'll have everything at once.' Mike looked at the list. 'What about carpets and curtains?'

'Well, I was going to cut down the curtains we had in High Walls. And they're going to leave the carpets in the bungalow—they'll do for a year or so.' As she spoke, she knew what he was going to say.

'No. Everything new, I think, unless there's something you're particularly attached to.'

'Not really. New stuff would be fun.'

'Good. Shall we buy it next Saturday? We'll have a day shopping in the big town. I'll pick you up at about eight.'

Angel seemed to be caught in an avalanche. 'All right,' she said.

'Look, I am not short of money. Most of the money I earned in the States I saved. And I earned a lot. I want this job done right so I can be assured that my niece is having the best.'

She was enjoying herself no end. They had ordered carpets, curtains, a vast amount of baby furniture. To her surprise, he didn't just let her make all the choices, he had his own point of view, too. They had started by selecting papers and colours for the rooms from a sheet of samples, and now were getting everything else to match.

They were spending a horrifying amount of money, but he didn't seem to mind. 'When we got the flat,' she said, 'we went out one morning and spent a hundred and fifty pounds and thought we were being mad, reckless and extravagant.' Then she caught herself. 'Sorry, that slipped out. Shouldn't have mentioned it.'

They were walking down the middle of a large and upmarket department store, surrounded by women in hats looking thoughtfully at Persian and Turkish rugs.

'Angel!' He stopped, grabbed her arms, shook her slightly. 'It happened! We were married! For a short time we had everything! All right, things went sour. But if we had the happiest days of our lives there, then we are entitled to remember them, no matter what went wrong later. Otherwise we deny part of what we are!'

'Happiest days of our lives? You never told me that then.' She was curious, not argumentative. 'I wish you had sometimes.'

He let go her arms, spoke in a quieter voice, and the ladies who had looked up returned to gazing at rugs. 'We never said much at all then,' he said. 'Life was good but it was hard. It was work, sleep and sex.'

'No, it was work, sleep and making love, Mike. There's a big difference. Now I think we'd better go down to the linen department.'

He didn't say anything until they'd walked down two floors into the basement. 'They *were* the happiest days of my life, Angel. What about you?'

'Who can tell?' she asked. She didn't want to tell the truth and say yes.

The next day they went to the bungalow and met Harold Days, the local builder. Angel had known him for years, had gone to school with his son. For a while they gossiped, exchanging local news while Mike stood by patiently. Harold asked about Janet's baby, Angel told him she had seen Terry.

'Good lad at heart,' Harold said judiciously, 'a determined little devil. He worked for me one summer, and I knew that I could set him going on a job, leave him for half a day and he'd still be at it when I came back. Hope he gets himself sorted out.'

'He will,' said Angel. 'He's got a stake in life now.'

'Are you coming to the meeting next Saturday? To object to closing the village school?'

'Oh, yes, I'll be there, it's got to be stopped. Now, can you work us out a price on what we want done'

Mr Days had been following them round, measuring and listening, scribbling furiously in his notebook, a much larger one than Mike's. 'I'll phone you through a price tomorrow,' he said.

'Thanks, Mr Days. If I pay cash, can you get all this work done in the next fortnight?'

Harold consulted his notebook, made a couple of calculations. 'Yes,' he said.

'When he's finished and your mother has recuperated, you can move in with your mother and Suzanne,' said Mike to Angel. 'A whole new life starting for you. I hope it'll be a contented one.'

CHAPTER FIVE

ANGEL had never quite realised how traumatic, how time consuming moving could be. Mr Martlett sent a couple of lads to help her move the heavier stuff out of High Walls and into the storeroom—there seemed to be plenty of it. Every day she called at the bungalow to see how the workmen were getting on, and what she saw made her even more excited at the prospect of moving in. Her life was altering. She hoped it was altering for the better.

She was spending as much time as she could with Suzanne. All the staff encouraged the mothers to bond with their babies, to spend as much time with them as was possible. So now she did what she had encouraged the mothers to do, nursing, crooning to the baby, holding her as much as possible. And she found a satisfaction greater than she had realised. For the first time she truly knew the meaning of the expression she had seen on mothers' faces.

It was Barry who gave her the greatest shock of all. 'You're becoming Suzanne's mother,' he said.

'That's silly, of course I'm not! She's just one of my charges and I—'

'Do you feel the same about all the rest in here?' he asked gently.

She had to give him an honest answer. 'No,' she said after a while.

'I thought not. Angel, I know you've been very busy recently. I've asked you out three times, each time you've given me a good reason for not coming. What I want to say is...I shan't ask again. We had one great evening, we're going to stay friends and work together, but that will be all. Are you all right with that?'

She sighed. 'Barry, I never wanted to hurt you. It was a great evening, but now my life seems to have changed and...and I do still want to be friends.'

'That's fine. Now, we've got other work to do.' He turned to look at the reports on their latest admission.

Angel didn't know what to think. She felt sad and guilty. Barry was a wonderful friend, that evening together had been good fun and she realised she had hurt him. But...that spark was missing. Barry would never be more than her friend. Perhaps it was as well to finish like this.

Mike came down to see the baby when he had time. Often she wasn't there, but the other nurses told her that he held the baby, cuddled her like any of the other fathers. He, too, was besotted.

On the Friday, after he had been to see Suzanne, he asked her how the work was progressing at the bungalow.

'It's going well, I'm really impressed. Most of the inside is finished. I've taken some of my stuff there already and I'm going to move in tomorrow night. D'you want to come up and look round?'

'I was hoping to, yes.'

She thought for a moment. 'There's a meeting at my old school at ten tomorrow that I want to go to, but it shouldn't last very long. D'you want to meet me at the bungalow at twelve?'

'Sounds ideal,' he said. 'I'm looking forward to seeing the place.'

* * *

She found it odd to go back to her old primary school. She had so many fond memories! And there were so many faces that she remembered. This had been a community school and the community was here. It didn't want its school to close.

They crowded into the main hall, some sitting at the little desks, others standing round the walls. After being welcomed by the head-teacher—a Mrs Simms—they were addressed by the chairman of the Save Our School committee, Miss Beavis.

Miss Beavis had been headmistress of the school for many years. After having to leave and taking a world cruise, she had come back as an unpaid assistant teacher. She still came in for three afternoons a week. She was now eighty-seven and as alert as she had been thirty years before.

'Children I have been proud to teach came from this school. We have produced doctors, architects, nurses, farmers, lawyers, no end of good mothers and fathers. Among many others I have two messages of support, from an old boy and an old girl. One is a government minister one is a vice admiral in the navy. And they tell us this school isn't financially viable. Rubbish!'

'That's a good argument,' a voice whispered from behind her.

She turned her head. To her surprise, there behind her was Mike. 'What are you doing here?' she whispered back, rather annoyed, 'I thought we arranged to meet later!'

'I found an extra couple of hours. Now, hush while I listen to this speech.'

What *was* he doing here? Mike never did anything without a definite motive. She wondered uneasily exactly what it might be.

After the speeches he wanted to look round the school where she had spent six formative years. They looked at the solid old stone building with BOARD SCHOOL written proudly above its front door. And there were three smaller portable classrooms, neatly arranged on the old playground. People were wandering round, meeting old schoolmates and reminiscing.

'I came here and I learned a lot,' said Angel. 'It's still a good school, supported by everybody around. They should judge a school by how well it does, not by how much money could be saved by closing it.'

'I agree. But education is like the health service. You count the cost before you do anything.' His voice was cynical.

'You don't really believe that?'

'No. But sometimes I think that every other medical manager does. Tell me more about growing up here. You never mentioned it before.'

'As we both agreed, we didn't do too much talking at all.' She pointed to the bell-tower on top of the main school. 'You see that slab of darker stone just below where the bell used to hang?'

He peered upwards. 'Yes? The one with some kind of mark on it?'

'That's something scratched on the stone. It says "Herbert Thwaite, 1923". My great-grandfather. He climbed up there when he was nine, and got very soundly smacked for it. He won a posthumous DCM in Africa in 1943, his name's on the memorial outside the church.'

He looked at her thoughtfully. 'You're telling me this for a reason, aren't you?'

'I'm trying to get you to understand something about belonging to a place. Shall we go and look at the bungalow now?'

He was impressed by what had been done. He peered at the new boiler, inspected the pile of baby stuff that had not yet been unpacked. The curtains and carpets were due to be fitted during the following week, but the place was beginning to look homely. Angel's bedroom already had her double bed in it, and she blushed when Mike glanced at the chaos of her dressing-table. There were things that still had to be put away.

Finally he stood in the conservatory, looking at the great vista of the valley below. 'This is why my mother will feel at home here,' she told him. 'She needs to feel she can breathe, have space.'

'I can almost understand.' For some reason his voice was harsh. 'She thinks this is better than nothing but chimneys, better than anything London can provide.'

'That's right,' she said, surprised at his apparent anger.

'So show me what's so wonderful, Angel. All I've done since I got here is work and take a trip shopping with you. I'm on call at seven tonight but till then I've got the afternoon off. So see if you can prove to me that this is better than a big city!'

It was a challenge. 'All right,' she said, 'I'll show you what this place means to me. We'll probably end up arguing, but I don't mind trying.'

He seemed to want to argue at once. 'You were happy enough in Buxton. And then you went even further—to South America.'

'I always knew I'd come back here,' she said quietly. 'I enjoyed wandering but this place was always home and I wanted to come back. When I was away I wrote every week, phoned whenever I could. I'm a local girl. I don't know how my brother managed to leave. I know he regrets it. And Ma…she just couldn't cope.'

He thought about this for a while. Then he changed the subject. 'I see. How is your mother? I gather that, since I've heard nothing, that she's doing all right.'

'She loves being with her grandchildren, and they love having her there. But she says the constant roar of traffic is getting her down.'

He looked across the valley. 'What about the constant bleating of sheep?' he asked, and she had to laugh.

They started by looking round the village. 'Do you know everyone?' he asked after a while. 'That's the tenth time you've said hello to someone.'

'I know a lot here. People tend not to move, or if they do move they come back. Like I did, in fact.'

She took him to see the memorial outside the church, showed him Herbert Thwaite's name. Then they went inside the church. 'Not locked?' he asked. 'A lot of churches have to be these days.'

'Someone will have seen us come in. If anyone looking a bit dubious went into the church, there'd be a phone call to the verger, or someone would come in after them. This is our church, we look after it. Mostly it was rebuilt in the nineteenth century, but there are bits of it that are much older.'

'I like it,' he said. She was pleased when she saw him put something in the box for the church restoration fund. She knew from their earlier life together that he wouldn't have done it unless he liked the building.

Outside again, she pointed to a tree at the bottom of the churchyard. 'My brother Martin broke his arm when he fell out of that tree. My mother said he shouldn't have been birds'-nesting anyway.'

'Obviously the Thwaites are a climbing family.'

'We are. But you'll have to do some climbing now. Do you still carry a pair of walking boots in your car?'

'You remember,' he said softly, and she looked away.

'I thought we'd go up on the moors,' she said to change the subject. She looked at the sky with an expert's eye. 'The weather's quite good and I think it should hold. Do you fancy a walk?'

'Part of the guided tour,' he said. 'I'd really like that. I've been stuck in the hospital for too long, I need to smell fresh air instead of antiseptic.'

'We'll get all the fresh air you want,' she said.

They went in her car, driving up past High Walls and then into the corner of a field where they could park. 'The main car park is at the top of the hill,' she said, 'a place called Pike's Ridge. This is a short cut.' Then she led him up the shoulder of a hill and onto the ridge. 'You asked for fresh air,' she said. 'Now you've got it.'

They could see for miles, a bleak but dramatic landscape of rolling moors with only the occasional sign of man. In the valley the wind had been gentle, intermittent. Here it blew steadily, chilling them after the exertion of climbing. Both buttoned up their anoraks. 'Believe it or not, this is an old Roman road,' she said, 'and it might be even older than that. These valleys were once full of forests.'

'And wild people like the Thwaites, who didn't like interlopers?'

'Probably. But we do accept the odd visitor. If he behaves himself.' She considered a minute. 'In fact, the Thwaites were probably interlopers themselves. It's a Viking name. The Vikings sailed up the river and then marched up here. Now, that's enough history.' She set off along the ridge path and he had to follow behind.

After half an hour they reached a high point, an outcrop of rocks standing high in the heather. She led him round the side, squeezed through a narrow passage between two tall rocks and there was the opening to a cave. 'Not a lot of people know this is here,' she said. 'They call it the smugglers' cave, though what smugglers were smuggling up here I don't know. I remember coming up here with my class and Miss Beavis once.'

'Quite a lady, Miss Beavis. I admired her performance this morning. Can we get in the cave? When I was a little boy I wanted to be a pirate and spend a lot of my time in caves.'

'If you want. It seems to get bigger inside.'

He stepped carefully down through the opening and then held out a hand to steady her. They were able to stand upright once inside. They didn't move, waiting for their eyes to acclimatise to the dark. He still held her hand and they were face to face, but all she could see of him was a vague blur.

'You didn't tell me anything about your childhood—about all this—when we were married,' he said. 'I would have liked to have known.'

It was easier to have a half-intimate conversation when they were in the dark. She didn't have to look at him, register the expression of his face. 'When you're younger different things are important,' she said. 'Remember what we agreed before—our life was work, sleep and—'

'Making love,' he supplied.

'You've got it right now. And after we'd made love I often wanted to talk, but all you wanted was more sleep!'

He laughed, sadly. 'I know. I'm sorry. I used to lie on my back. And after a while you'd lean over me, you'd giggle a bit and then you'd brush your breasts across my face. It was...'

'It was what?'

'Well, it certainly stopped me sleeping.'

The memory flashed into her mind, so strong it might have been yesterday. Suddenly she could feel the warmth of his body, the gentle rasping of his beard on her face, that infinitely exciting smell that meant they had been together.

She could still see nothing of his face. But his voice, the very way his body was next to hers, told her that he was remembering as she was. 'Well, we'd better get out and walk a bit more,' she gabbled. 'There's another main road about four miles away and—'

He took her in his arms and kissed her. The shock was so great that she gave in at once. And then she responded, holding him to her as he clutched her. She didn't know what she was feeling—it was an odd mixture of sensations, both familiar and strange. But she loved it.

For a while they kissed. Then she felt his hand at her back, sliding under her anorak and sweater, tugging at her shirt, feeling the warmth of her skin. In a moment he might... She had to stop this...but she would wait just a few seconds more.

It was so hard to do. Gently she pushed him away, stepped back a little.

'We must stop now, Mike,' she whispered. 'There are so many memories coming back and I couldn't stand the pain again.'

'I like kissing you so much.'

There was no way she could hide the truth, she had just fully realised it herself. 'And I like kissing you. It's not just the kissing, it's because it's you. Mike, I've tried so hard not to let things start again between us. But it's no use, I can feel...feel what we had creeping back. And I got hurt so much!'

Slowly he released her and there was only silence in the cave. The vagueness of his figure loomed above her; to one side a thin streak of sunlight illuminated the cave floor.

'Perhaps,' he said, after what seemed liked an eternity, 'perhaps you can never recapture the past exactly. Life moves on. But I would like you to be part of my future. What now?'

'Now I need time to think. Shall we carry on with the walk?'

'It's the reason we came here,' he said. 'You get out first.'

Walking was different after that. The path was broader here and they walked side by side. There was no excuse for not talking to him. But Angel couldn't get over the excitement of his kiss and the truth that had been torn from her. What was she to do now?

Mike appeared equally puzzled. She thought he might be feeling exactly the same way. Surely he knew exactly what he wanted?

Desperately she cast about for something to say.

'Tell me about your family,' she said. 'We never talked about our families at all.' Then she paused. Perhaps this subject would pain him. But, in fact, he seemed ready, even eager to talk.

'I think I had told you my family was of no consequence when we met,' he said. 'I believe I told you that they wouldn't interfere with us.' His face was set like stone. 'In fact, all I had was my sister—about four years younger than me. Our parents were both killed in a gas explosion when we were very young—I have no memory of them whatsoever. My father had an older—a much older—sister who said she could take Monica but not me. I don't think she really wanted Monica. Anyway, I went to an orphanage. When I got older I tried to get in touch but the aunt had died and Monica was starting on the third of a set of foolish relationships. I learned very quickly not to interfere. We exchanged Christmas cards, that was all. Then I got this new job and out of the blue Monica phoned. She wanted to come to see me.'

'Did she want to get to know you again?' Angel asked curiously. 'D'you think she was hoping for some kind of reconciliation?'

'I suppose that was possible, I'd certainly like to think so. But I suspect she just wanted to borrow more money. She'd done it before. I would have sent her some, I have in the past, but...but now she's dead.'

'That's a sad story,' Angel said. 'Apart from Suzanne, you're now completely alone.'

'Being alone isn't too bad. Having relations has only ever meant trouble. Look at me and you.'

'We had our moments,' she said, thinking that that was a mammoth understatement.

'I know we did, Angel. And now I have Suzanne to love.'

Angel didn't ask him if the love of a child was enough. Perhaps she didn't want to know the answer.

After that they talked of less troublesome things, of the running of Micklekirk hospital and how it was better than most. They enjoyed the rest of the walk and then she drove him back to the bungalow. Then she remembered why they had been walking the first place.

'I've showed you round a bit of my background and history,' she said. 'Do you understand now what it all means to me?'

'I think so,' he said carefully. 'I can see you love this place. The trouble is, love so often goes sour. What will you be left with if it does?'

'It won't go sour,' she said confidently.

She felt relaxed with him now, so much so that she asked him if he'd like to stay to tea. There were some rooms habitable in the bungalow, and she had brought plenty of food. They had a cup of tea together and then she left him in the living room while she cooked. When Angel went back after ten minutes to ask if he wanted more tea, he was asleep in the rocking chair. She smiled and left him.

At twenty past seven she heard Mike's mobile ring and then there was the mutter of his voice. He came into the kitchen at once, rubbing his face.

'Well, I suppose I am on call,' he said. 'It's my senior reg—we're going to have to open a chest. A farmer's just been sent up from A and E. Apparently he was working under a vehicle when it slipped and crushed him. The SR thinks he can cope but he wouldn't mind if I was standing by. I'm afraid I'm going to have to miss tea, Angel.'

She indicated the array of pans on the stove. 'Tea's far from ready yet and I'm not very hungry. If you want to...why don't you come back when you've finished? This will all keep warm.'

He smiled. 'I'd like that, Angel. See you later.'

For a moment she wondered if he would kiss her, just a gentle kiss on the cheek perhaps. There was something about the way he was looking at her, as if he wanted to. But he didn't. He turned and left.

Mike drove out of Laxley village, down the hill towards Micklekirk Hospital. He wasn't happy with himself. This situation was ridiculous!

He had come to Micklekirk almost expecting a rest. For years he had worked and trained in America; he had learned certain techniques there that no one else in Britain could perform. Others were in America training now, but he was the first, the one who was expected to take the chair in a prestigious London hospital. It was what he had worked towards for so long!

Working at Micklekirk was supposed to be easy. In fact, he had found an excellent team of co-workers and a very demanding workload. No matter, he liked work. But his personal life…

The first shock had been the death of his sister. He could have coped with this; he knew she had no regard for him and that she was only interested in what money she could get from him. In the past he had tried so hard to become close to her and it had always ended badly. Even though she had been his only living relative, he couldn't honestly shed much of a tear for Monica.

And, as ever, she had left him in more trouble. He was the only living relative of a baby. This he didn't want; he'd had enough of family responsibilities! Well, that had been his first reaction. His second reaction had startled even him. He'd looked at this tiny scrap of humanity who was his only living blood relative and—he loved her! When he looked down at her he felt emotions that had been dormant since…since he had thought he was to be a father. He loved her. And he wouldn't be parted from her.

And now the biggest problem. Angel. The woman he was once married to. Looking back, he seemed to have been a different man then. They had both been different, thinking of only two things—their work for most of the twenty-four hours, each other for the rest. Then work had come between them.

He realised that he had cut himself off from his feelings, had worked with an intensity that now bothered him. Uneasily he wondered if he had lost something. He was happy, proud of his accomplishments, he had an international reputation. But was he happy?

He had never asked himself that question before.

He drove into the car park, hastened up to the cardiac centre. His senior reg was waiting there. 'Things are a bit more complex than I thought,' he said.

CHAPTER SIX

THERE was a full team waiting—anaesthetist, scrub nurse, assistants, SHO and the SR himself. As Mike showered, dressed in greens and scrubbed up, he listened to the SR's report. Of course, he would examine the records himself, But an initial overview was always a useful thing to have.

'Name's Jake Lauren,' the SR said, 'a farmer from further down the valley, aged thirty-seven. He had this heavy trailer jacked up, he was lying on his back underneath it, greasing one of the axles. It wasn't the right jack for the job and it slipped.'

'Now, there's a surprise for us all,' said Mike. The number of injuries that came into A and E because someone hadn't been using the right lifting tool was enormous.

'I've had a word with the family. Apparently he's in good health, very fit, no history of heart trouble, doesn't smoke. His chest wasn't crushed for long—there was someone nearby who jacked up the trailer and got him straight out. They called an ambulance at once. He was still conscious but in severe pain and complained of not being able to breathe. Consciousness was altered also.'

'Classic,' said Mike. 'Do you think the heart is lacerated or just contused?'

The SR said he wasn't certain. Mike was glad. Although you might suspect what was wrong, he knew there could be no way of knowing fully until the chest was opened. He didn't want an over-confident assistant.

'Investigations?' he asked.

'I found hypotension, distended neck veins, paradoxical pulses. Radiography, ECG, echocardiogram all suggest cardiac tamponade and possible disruption of the vena cavae.'

'Good,' said Mike. I'll have a look at them all and have a quick word with the man and his family. Then we'll get started.'

'There's a message for you, sir,' said one of the porters, 'which was only to be given to you when you'd quite finished. It's not urgent, not bad news, but will you, please, ring the neonatal unit?'

Not bad news. So Suzanne wasn't ill or anything like that. He rang the unit. He recognised the voice of the nurse who replied—he'd spoken to her once or twice. 'Mr Gilmour? Can you hold on a minute? We've got someone who wants to speak to you. At the moment she's asleep in our parents' room.' Then there was a giggle and a moment later a sleepy voice said, 'Mike? It's Angel.'

Of course, he had said he would be back for tea after a couple of hours. 'Angel! It's two o'clock in the morning, I thought you would have guessed—things were a lot worse than we anticipated.'

'I'm a nurse, remember. I know how operations can change. In fact, I phoned up the theatre and they explained what was happening. How was it, by the way?'

'I think a success,' he said carefully. 'You never know what might happen—but I'm pleased with what we managed.'

'That's good. Mike, I'm so glad.' He could tell by the warmth in her voice that she meant it and it pleased him. 'Now, I baked a quiche for you in my new oven and I really wanted you to try it. So I thought I'd come down here and wait for you and try to persuade you to come back and see if you liked it. Then things went on and I decided to sleep. By the way, how d'you feel?'

How did he feel? 'My nerves are jangling,' he said honestly. 'I'm tired but there's no way I could sleep for a while. It was just an ordinary operation—not a simple one, quite complex really, but I'd done it before and I thought it went well.'

'I remember when you used to work a late night, sometimes you'd wake me up and tell me all about it.'

'Yes, and you never complained,' he said thoughtfully. 'You'd always look interested and listen.'

'It seems like it's happening again. I didn't think you'd be this long, but if you still want to come back to the bungalow and eat, it's all ready and waiting. Of course, you might be better off in your bed.'

'I'm coming,' he said. 'I've just realised I'm ravenous. I'll have a quick word with the family, then a shower and I'll see you outside in fifteen minutes.'

'We'll take my car,' she said. 'You're not safe to drive.'

He had been up for twenty hours.

Angel quite liked eating with Mike at this odd hour of the morning. He didn't want the beer or wine she offered him, just water. Working for hours under those lights tended to dehydrate him. For a while she listened while he talked about what he had just done. She understood that it was a relief from tension, a way of calming down.

They finished the meal then she cleared away while he sat in the rocking chair again. 'Tea or coffee?' she asked.

'No. They're not what I want,' he said.

He was dressed in shirt and jeans, the outfit he had worn when they'd gone for their walk. His hair was slicked down after the shower he'd had, and his cheeks were darkened—it was a while since he'd shaved. His blue eyes were tired, but in them she recognised a spark that flared in her, too. And how well she remembered those lips. As he stood he swayed slightly.

'What do you want, then?' she asked. She knew the answer to the question but she had to hear him say it.

'I want you.' A simple, stark answer.

Just for a moment she hesitated. Then she walked towards him, put her arms round that firm waist. 'Then you can have me,' she said.

For a while they just stood there in the living room, their bodies pressed together. Even though they were both dressed it seemed that she could feel all of him, her calves, thighs, hips, breasts all touching him, filling her with desire. When he kissed her it was so gentle at first that she sighed, it was like a spell turning her body to liquid. She had to lie down.

With her arm around his waist she urged him to her bedroom. He kissed her more passionately now, but she stopped him. She loosened his belt, pulled his shirt over his head as if her were a child. Then she pushed down his jeans so that he stood naked before her. 'Lie on my bed,' she said. 'Lie on my bed and wait.'

He did as she told him, unashamed of his nakedness, unashamed of his obvious need for her. She pulled off her own clothes quickly—

they must be equal as soon as possible. Then she stepped to the bed and knelt astride him.

'Do you remember this?' she asked. Leaning forward, she trailed her breasts across his face, letting their fullness touch his cheeks, his lips. She could feel the roughness of his growing beard. The tiny pain hardened her nipples, made them full, as excited as she was.

He sighed underneath her, wrapped an arm round her shoulders and crushed her breasts to his face. Then he pulled her head to his and his kiss now was hard, demanding, a response to equal his own desire.

They remained locked there together and her body rested on his, feeling the fire of his skin.

Then slowly he rolled her onto her back. To her this now seemed entirely proper, the thing they should do. All other thoughts had left her. She knew only that she wanted to give herself to this man. She spread her body out beneath him, felt him pause, knew he was looking down at her. She heard him catch his breath, a sound almost like a sob. Then she took him to her.

It was half remembered, half new and all wonderful. It didn't last long. There was no time for gentleness, just a craving that both needed to satisfy. And then a joint cry, and it was over. He lay on his back now, pulled her half on top of him with her head on his shoulder, his arms round her. And in no time he was asleep. She had no time to think, she didn't want to think. She pulled the duvet over them both and soon she too slept.

Angel woke early. For some time she lay still, forcing herself not to think about the warmth of the body next to hers, the deep breathing and the relaxed hand that lay so casually on her waist. Then cautiously she slid out of bed, took her clothes from where she had dropped them and walked into the next room. She dressed quickly, then sat at the kitchen table to write the letter she had already planned.

Dear Mike,

I have gone for a walk round the village. When you wake take my car to drive back to hospital. Leave the car by the babies' unit and put the key on the front wheel.

Last night was so lovely but it was also a dreadful mistake. I am sorry, I know it was my fault, but if you think anything of me, please never mention it again. I don't want to talk about us or our past. Can we carry on as friends and colleagues, as we were before?

Yours, Angel.

She tiptoed into the bedroom and, carefully avoiding looking at his face, left the note on the pillow. Then she took her coat and walked out into the village.

What had happened between them? Was it sex, or love, or sex and love combined? She just didn't know. She walked round the village, trying to decide how she felt. Making love with Mike had been so wonderful that it threatened to displace everything else. But she couldn't let that take place. Look what had happened the last time. They had parted because they hadn't been able to get their two lives to work together. It would be even harder now.

When Angel got back to the bungalow her car was still outside. She turned and went for another half-hour's walk. After that the car was still there. She was angry now. If he wanted a confrontation he could have one. But he wasn't there. Instead there was a note on the kitchen table.

Dear Angel,

Thanks for the offer of the car, but I think I also need a walk.

Last night was wonderful. I was happier than ever I have been in my life before. Now I will never mention it again unless you do first.

I would have thought that we did have things we had to discuss, but this I will leave to you. In the past you have accused me of making decisions on my own. Now you must do it.

Please forgive me if I sign this,

All my love, Mike.

Well, he had always been able to write a good letter. She tried to get on with her work in the bungalow. But as she worked the tears ran down her face.

Next day Angel was told by the paediatric consultant that Suzanne would soon be ready to leave the hospital. 'I know about the…sad circumstances of this case,' Linda said, 'but we'll still have to know what arrangements Mr Gilmour is making for Suzanne's future.'

Angel took a deep breath. 'Mr Gilmore is going to keep Suzanne,' she said. 'In time she'll move down to London with him. But until that happens she'll stay with me or with Nancy Timms. I'll be taking some of my holiday time soon to get things settled.'

'I see,' said the consultant, who obviously didn't see. 'It's a lot to take on, no one knows that better than you, Angel. Does this mean that you and Mr Gilmour are...?'

'No, we're not. This is a purely temporary arrangement. We're just helping each other out.'

'Well, you know how demanding a baby can be. Having said that, Angel, there is no one I would rather discharge a baby to.' She frowned. 'There will be quite a few formalities to see to and I suppose Social Services will have to be consulted. More forms to fill in!'

'I know Judy Harris, the children's social worker, quite well,' Angel said thoughtfully. 'We've had plenty of dealings with her in the past. We should be able to get something satisfactory sorted out.'

'I'm sure we shall. I'll phone both her and Mr Gilmour and then see if we can set up a case conference. Can you arrange for Nancy Timms to come in, too?'

The building and decorating work on the inside of the bungalow were finished, much earlier than expected, then on one day the curtains arrived and on the second the carpets were fitted. She laid out all the baby requirements in the little room she had decided would be the nursery. It was different from doing it in a ward, she felt far more personally involved. This was going to be *her* baby.

Angel had only seen Mike at a distance in the past few days. But they met the paediatric consultant just before the social worker arrived for the conference. To her relief he treated her in the same friendly way they had treated each other before *that* night.

'I hadn't realised that doing a simple thing like looking after a family was so complex,' he said, 'but I guess we have to put up with it. Good of you to go through all this, Angel.'

There was a questioning look in his eyes, but she ignored it. 'I'm sure we're all happy with the situation as it is,' she said. 'It seems to suit all parties well.'

Judy Harris arrived with Nancy Timms—the two were old friends—and seemed equally happy. 'For once I'm happy to cut corners,' Judy said. 'This seems an arrangement that benefits everybody. Suzanne here is a very lucky baby. Now, all I need are vast numbers of forms filled in. Angel, I'll have to make a visit to both the new homes, and I'll be visiting again, as will as the district nurse. Are you happy with that?'

'Come whenever you want. You know you'll always be welcome.'

So it was quickly done. 'Perfect,' Linda said. 'I'll be looking at Suzanne in a couple of weeks and regularly after that, but for now she can be discharged. Friday be all right, Angel?'

It was suddenly all very, very near. She gulped. 'Friday will be fine,' she said.

In the past she had seen parents come in to take their babies home for the first time from the neonatal unit. Often they had been nervous, unhappy, not sure that they could cope. Angel and the rest of the team had done their best to encourage and support. Now she was taking a baby home. There could be few people better qualified than she was. And yet she found herself as nervous as anyone.

There were specific rules about handing over a baby. Before letting any parent take a child from the neonatal unit, the staff had to be certain that the parents or guardians knew how to look after the child. Even though Angel was a children's nurse, and Linda Patterson had known her for years, Linda still came down to have a couple of words before baby Suzanne was discharged on Friday. Another nurse carried the baby out of the hospital, Angel wasn't allowed to. Now she was guardian, not nurse.

It should have been easy. Suzanne wasn't her child. There was no blood bond linking them. But over the past weeks Angel had fallen in love with the little girl. Suzanne had a character, Angel could respond to it. She knew the two of them would get on together.

While they were going through the necessary procedures, Mike came into the ward. 'Just dropped in to see that everything was all right,' he said. 'Tell me if I'm in the way and I'll go.'

'You're not at all in the way,' Angel said. 'It's good to see you here. I was going to phone you. If you have the time, would you like to come home with us? See how things are going, watch her being fed. In fact, you can feed her. Suzanne will stay with me for the next couple of weeks.'

'I'd very much like that,' he said quietly, 'but I need to be sure that I wouldn't be a nuisance. Wouldn't upset you in any way.'

Another coded message. 'You won't upset me,' she told him. 'I've looked after babies all my professional life. I can cope with you easily.'

So he drove up after her, watched as she put the baby to bed in the new nursery. Suzanne cried, but that was to be expected. Afterwards Angel took him on a quick tour to see the curtains, the carpets, the way she had tried to make the bungalow a home.

'It's just what we need,' she said, 'and my mother will be coming back on Sunday. She's feeling much better and really looking forward to looking after Suzanne.'

He frowned. 'Well, I'm very pleased about that,' he said, 'but as her surgeon I know that the time between now and after she's had her operation will be just the time when she can't really cope.'

'No problem. Nancy's only down the road.'

After a while he had to leave, and she was left alone with the baby.

It seemed odd to be on her own and working. For the first time her personal and her working life were mixed. Later in the evening Angel bathed the baby, fed her again and then put her back in her cot. She made herself a quick meal and sat down to watch television. She felt restless. It's just the novelty, she told herself, just the mixture of home life and work. But something seemed to be missing. Perhaps it was her mother.

She went to bed with the cot by her bedside, but she couldn't sleep. Like so many of the mothers she had observed, she was fascinated by the sound of the baby's breathing. There was something calming about it. But she still couldn't sleep.

She had used the new washing machine that Mike had bought for her. Two nights after the night with him she had stripped off the sheets and thrown them in the dirty linen basket. When she had climbed into bed the next night, there had been the faintest of scents there, not of her but him. In the middle of the night she had risen, torn off the sheets and replaced them. She couldn't sleep, tantalised by that living memory.

This bed, this room, this house were all so much more comfortable than High Walls. But it was hours before she slept.

At four in the morning she had to wake to feed and change Suzanne. No problem to this, she had done it so many times before. Afterwards Suzanne wouldn't go back to sleep. Angel rocked her, cuddled her, walked with her. Still the crying. So Angel did what she had sometimes recommended to her new mums.

She lay on her back on the bed, put the baby between her breasts and let her rest there. Quite quickly Suzanne went to sleep. Angel felt her hunting for a while, felt the tiny hands on her naked breasts.

This was something she had never done before—she had nursed many babies when she was clothed, but never this most intimate of contacts. Suzanne couldn't suckle, of course, but she tried. It was the oddest of feelings. Angel remembered the peaceful, happy faces of her nursing mums. She knew why, of course, it was just one effect of prolactin—a hormone produced by the pituitary gland to make milk flow. But she found she loved the feeling herself. When she put the sleeping baby back in her cot she found tears running down her face. Just tired, she told herself.

Her mother came back on Sunday afternoon and settled into Valley View at once. Mike came out to see her, he said both as her doctor and as the guardian of his child. He took her into the bedroom for a quick examination and said that the stay down South had done her no end of good.

Angel thought she hadn't seen her mother so happy in months. She sat in the rocking chair and fed Suzanne as Mike and Angel had a quiet word in the kitchen.

'She's still not a hundred per cent fit, Angel,' said Mike quietly. 'Make sure she keep up with her medication, and don't let her do too much. Use Nancy as much as you like. And I'd like to see her in hospital later in the week. I'll consider bringing her operation forward a little.'

'You're frightening me,' she said. 'Are you saying that there's something seriously wrong with her?'

'No, I'm not saying that. But remember, there's always the tenth of one per cent chance that something might go wrong. And that tenth of one per cent means one in every thousand people.'

'I'll look after her.'

So when Angel went back to work on Monday morning she felt a little apprehensive at leaving her mother behind. But Ma was more than happy and Nancy was going to call round and stay for most of the day.

'Are you missing High Walls?' asked Angel.

'No. I've started a new life here.'

What sort of a new life have I started? Angel wondered to herself.

CHAPTER SEVEN

SOMETIMES he was delayed because of work, but otherwise Mike came every evening. After Angel had showed him how—Suzanne was still tiny—he would feed the little girl, bathe her, dress her and hold her before putting her into her cot.

He had a surgeon's delicacy and dexterity and Angel knew at once that Suzanne would be safe in his hands. But she liked to sit and watch as, absorbed, he tended his little girl.

Late on Friday afternoon it was raining, blowing half a gale, another typical late winter night on the moors. As she moved from warm kitchen to equally warm and draught-proof living room, Angel thought of High Walls ands shivered. This was the way to live!

The phone rang. She thought it would be Mike, he usually phoned to say if he would be delayed. But to her surprise it was Mr Martlett. He sounded worried. 'Angel, have you got a minute to talk to me? There's a problem—a big one—and you might be able to help.'

'You couldn't have been more thoughtful over High Walls. Anything I can do to help you, I will.'

He sighed. 'I'm not the one in trouble, I'm afraid. You know Terry Blackett? I gather you've seen him and his baby from time to time.'

'I've known Terry since primary school. Why? Is the baby all right?'

'The baby is fine. Terry isn't. I'm at the police station, Angel. They've called me in as they think I might be able to help. And I will if I can but—'

'Just tell me what happened,' she said. 'Then we'll see if I can help.'

'Terry was allowed out again, on his own, to see his baby. Part of this new scheme they're trying. He had left the hospital and was walking through the rain to catch the bus. An old Land Rover apparently deliberately swerved across the road to splash him—there was a witness in a car behind, that's how we know all this. Anyway, the Land Rover stopped, someone in it leaned out and jeered at Terry.'

'Not a good idea,' said Angel. 'Terry can't control his temper.'

'He didn't. He got to the car, pulled someone out of the passenger side and thumped him. There was a bit of a mix-up, another man from the car joined in the fight, it was hard to see. Then a shotgun was fired. We think Terry was hurt.'

'You *think* he was hurt? Don't you know?'

'No, we don't. You know Terry's a big, strong lad. Apparently he flattened both these two louts in the car. Well, someone had phoned the police. They arrived in a car, lights flashing, siren blaring. Terry panicked. He fired the shotgun at the police car, then got in the Land Rover and drove off.'

'It wasn't his fault!' Angel cried. 'Anyone can see he was provoked he didn't know what he was doing!'

'We know that. The police see it as a convicted criminal firing at a police vehicle and then going on the run. Apparently there were more shells in the Land Rover. Anyway, the police followed the vehicle onto the moors and

Terry abandoned it at Pike's Ridge, got out and ran. Now there's a big police operation in progress. Men with guns are going to try to surround him, they think he might shoot someone.'

'If Terry sees men with guns hunting him, he'll panic more,' Angel said decisively. 'He's likely to fire back. All they need do is leave him alone. He'll turn himself in in time.'

'They daren't risk that with a man with a gun. I just phoned you on the off chance that you might have some idea where he'd go. If I could talk to him perhaps…'

'Pick me up here in ten minutes,' she said. 'We'll go up onto the moors ourselves.'

She briefly explained the situation to her mother, who said she'd look after Suzanne. Then she changed into her hard weather clothes, packed a torch, some chocolate and a small first-aid outfit. She was ready when Sam Martlett arrived in his four-wheel drive.

When they got near Pike's Ridge they found a police car drawn across the road. At Sam's insistence a constable took them to a large van fitted as an office. From inside it a Superintendent Wragg was directing the operation. Through the rain Angel could see other cars further on, with some policemen in hard hats and bulletproof vests, carrying guns. She shivered.

'We might need your help,' said the superintendent. 'It could be useful when we've got him pinned down. We have sent for our own negotiator and until we have something more to go on I'll have to ask you keep well away.'

'You know he panicked,' Angel shouted. 'All this is making things worse. If you just go away he'll come to you.'

'Possibly. But we daren't take that risk with a man with a loaded gun. I'm sorry, miss, I'll have to ask you to wait here. I'll send for you if I think we need you.'

She thought the man sounded sympathetic, but she knew he was right. It was a risk no policeman dared take. 'You stay with the superintendent,' she said to Sam. 'I'll drive your car down the road a way.'

He handed her the keys. 'We have to do what the police say,' he said. She nodded and went to his vehicle.

She only knew afterwards what happened next. So far the police had only gathered, they hadn't started their hunt yet. Sam was talking to the superintendent when a constable came up and said, 'Excuse me, sir, we've just seen a woman in a red anorak running across the moor towards the ridge. What would you like us to do?'

The superintendent turned to Sam. 'This is that nurse woman of yours, isn't it? Doesn't she know how to obey orders?'

'Not really,' Martlett said calmly. 'She'll do as she thinks best. And before you ask, no, I didn't know this was what she was going to do.'

The superintendent could hardly contain his anger. 'Doesn't she know she's jeopardising an entire operation? I'll have her arrested for this!'

'You'd better catch her first. Now, you may not want it, but this is my advice. Don't try to stop her. If Terry Blackett is on those moors, watching you, and he sees his friend being dragged away by your men, he's not going to be very happy. He might even try to rescue her. And you wouldn't want that.'

For a moment the two men stared at each other. Then the superintendent said to the patiently waiting constable, 'Don't do anything, Kenton. Tell the others.'

'Sir!' The man disappeared.

'I hope you know what you're doing,' the superintendent said.

'So do I,' said Sam.

Angel ran through the heather, her heart thudding, her chest heaving, the wet plants catching at her ankles. She knew she'd be seen pretty soon, that she only had a short start. But it might be enough. She had to get to Terry first. He just couldn't cope with large numbers of people. She remembered even at school how he'd hated crowds, how they'd made him uneasy. If he could just get his cottage, with his wife and child and sheep to look after. If she could get to him first.

She looked over her shoulder. The police were there, in the distance, now coming towards her along the ridge. But they didn't seem to be moving too quickly. If she could just maintain her lead. If she was right about where Terry might be. If Terry would listen to her.

Eventually she reached the little rock outcrop where she had stopped with Mike, the outcrop where there was the smugglers' cave. This was her only hope. She pulled herself onto a rock, tried to signal to the advancing men in rain-stained blue uniforms that they were to stay back. Perhaps they slowed a little. All she needed was a little time.

It was surprisingly difficult to find the entrance to the cave. When she slid between the two tall rocks she realised that there was little daylight left and darkness would come soon. That would make things even more tricky. And someone had cleverly pulled stones and bracken round the little cleft in the rocks. You needed to know the cave was there. But there would be policemen who knew.

She pulled at the stones in the entrance of the cave and shouted, 'Terry! It's me, Angel Thwaite! Don't shoot, Terry, it's me—Angel.'

There was no reply. Two thoughts struck her. Perhaps Terry wasn't there. And if he was, perhaps he was angry enough, desperate enough, to shoot her. It was the first time this had crossed her mind.

She wasn't backing out now. She stepped into the darkness, her hands outstretched in front of her. 'Terry, are you there? I've got to talk to you before the police come.'

The voice was so close that she screamed. 'Angel? What are you doing here? You've brought them here after me. I thought you was my friend.'

She listened to his voice. It was high, fluttering, as if hysteria was not far away. The last thing Terry needed now was excitement.

'Terry, they were coming here anyway. Now, I've got a torch here. I want to look at your arm. I've brought some—'

'No! You leave and they might follow you. Then I can slip away and—'

'Terry, we're surrounded. No one's going to slip away and I'll be in trouble for coming to try to help you. Now, I'm going to switch the torch on and look at your arm.'

She switched on the torch she had decided to bring. Terry was a sorry sight. He was wearing a light raincoat, now sodden with the rain and stained after his flight through the heather. His hair was matted and his face unnaturally white. A scarf was wrapped round his left arm, above the elbow.

In his right hand he held the shotgun. He was a countryman so he held it broken, safe. But it would be too easy to snap it together again.

'Take your coat and jacket off, Terry. I need to see that arm. You've lost blood already, you'll probably need a transfusion.'

'Where will I get one of those?'

'In hospital, Terry. That's where you'll be going ultimately. I can't deal with a gunshot wound here. Now, coat and jacket off!'

He placed the gun behind him—within easy reach, she noticed. Then, his face twitching with the pain, he pulled off the coat and jacket. He was shivering.

'We'll have to get you into something warm and dry,' she said matter-of-factly, 'otherwise you might get pneumonia as well. Here...' From her pocket she took a bar of chocolate and handed it to him. 'Eat this. You'll feel better.'

As best she could, she cleaned up the wounds on his upper arm. Two pellets had cut through the flesh which would at some time have to be sutured. She was pretty sure that two more were still embedded deep in the flesh.

'Terry, you've been shot. You're in a bad way, you've got to see a doctor!'

'In a bad way! Not as bad as those following me.' He reached for the gun, snapped it closed.

'Terry! Those policemen have done nothing to you, a couple of them know you. Now, break that gun again and sit here by me.'

He did as she asked. After a moment he said, 'Would you like a piece of this chocolate? I'm sorry I didn't share it.'

She thought she would burst into tears. This was Terry twenty-odd years ago, the boy who would share everything.

'I've got more chocolate here if I need it,' she said. 'Terry, what are you going to do now?'

His smile was ghastly. 'Well I've missed my train back to prison so I guess I'm in trouble. Might as well make a fight of it.'

'Don't be silly. You're in trouble but things could get worse. Mr Martlett is out there, he wants you to come out. He's not asking through charity, he thinks you're the best shepherd for miles. And what about Jackie and your baby? What is she going to think of this? Your mother says you're going to get married.'

'When? Angel, I'm going to spend the rest of my life in prison! And I can't stand it. I'd rather be dead than go back to be locked up there.'

His mood seemed to alternate between reasonable and hysterical. She knew this was probably a result of shock, blood loss and the run along the ridge. He needed urgent medical help—but he wanted to fight.

'I think we can sort something out,' she said, 'if you—'

Suddenly, the entrance to the cave was floodlit. He grabbed the gun again, snapped it shut. 'I'll shoot that light out, I'll—'

'No you won't. I'll go and see what I can do.' Feeling both foolish and frightened, she put her hands high over her head, then stepped into the beam. ' Don't shoot! Can you see me? I'm Angel Thwaite.'

'We can see you, miss. Are you alone in there?' The sound of another voice upset her, the man sounded so normal.

'No, I'm in here with Terry Blackett. We're having a talk. Now, this is the only opening to the cave. He can't escape. That light is disturbing us. Can you turn it out?'

'I don't think so.'

'Look, we're both all right. We can sort this out if you just take your mates with guns away.'

She had seen it all on TV. The thought that there were men nearby with their guns trained on her, or near her, was horrible. And it wasn't necessary.

'Just wait a minute,' the voice called. 'We can turn it down. Would Terry like to talk to someone? We've got someone here.'

'He's got someone to talk to,' she said tartly. 'Me. Now, leave us alone.' A minute later the bright light dimmed. She went back into the cave.

She knew that Terry must be weakening fast. But there was a glassy look in his eyes and she wondered if he might try to do something heroic, or stupid, before he fell unconscious.

'They've got someone to talk to you,' she said. 'I wonder who it could be. The only person I can see doing any good is Miss Beavis.'

Then it happened. He laughed. 'Miss Beavis! I liked her. She didn't half smack me, but she never made me cry. I took what was coming to me.'

'Yes, you did. So are you going to cry now?'

This was it, she felt, her last chance of getting through to him. The silence between them went on and on. She shivered herself, became conscious of her own wet hair, of the unpleasant trickle down her spine, of the damp in her boots.

'So what do I do?' he asked.

'Give me the gun and the shells and I'll take them out. Then you come out with your arms over your head. They'll grab you, hold you on the ground and handcuff you. Don't fight back.' Once again, she had seen all this on television.

'Sounds just like shearing a sheep,' he said. 'Angel, my little girl—'

'I told you I'd keep an eye on her and I will. Now, pass me the gun and the shells.'

He had made up his mind now. He broke the gun, slipped out two shells. It had been loaded! She had wondered. Then he handed her the shotgun and took a box of shells from behind him. 'That's the lot,' he said.

She went to the entrance and shouted, 'I'm coming out with the gun in my hand. Don't shoot.'

Suddenly the light was bright again. The voice said, 'Keep coming forward then put the gun on the ground and step back.' She did as she was told. Someone rushed up and took the gun, then she walked forward.

There was a group of men in shiny coats there. She gave one the box of shells and said. 'He's coming out with his hands up. He hasn't got a gun. He realises he made a mistake and he certainly doesn't want anyone hurt so keep those guns down. He also needs hospital treatment quite quickly.'

She turned, and there was Terry behind her. 'Sheep-shearing time,' he said, and fell to his knees.

Angel was taken, politely but firmly, a little distance from Terry. The police did handcuff him but she was pleased to see that they weren't as rough with him as they might have been. Sam Martlett was standing nearby, and he had a quick word with Terry.

It was now quite dark. The scene was lit by torches carried by the police, which shone eerily on their shiny wet coats. And the rain still slanted down.

'We appear to have more or less a happy ending,' Superintendent Wragg said to her. 'But, Miss Thwaite, you interfered with a police—'

'That can wait till later,' a voice snarled. 'There's no need for it now. Anyway, she saved you from a very nasty job. Angel, are you sure you're absolutely all right?'

What was Mike doing here? He sounded very angry. 'I'm wet and a bit cold,' she told him, 'but I'm all right. Mike, can you look at Terry's arm? It looked as if…'

It obviously took him an effort to be calm and polite, but Mike turned to the Superintendent and said, 'My name's Mike Gilmour. I'm a surgeon. Would you like me to have a quick look at that man? He appears to have been hurt.'

'We have a paramedic handy, but I'd be obliged,' said the superintendent. 'After all, this appears to be amateur night.'

Mike walked over to Terry who was now sitting on a rock. He looked at his eyes, checked his pulse, asked a couple of low questions. 'Don't undo that dressing on his arm,' Angel called. 'I've just put it on. But I think there are pellets still inside him.' Mike turned and nodded.

'He'd better go to A and E,' he said to the superintendent, 'but otherwise he's reasonably fit.'

'In that case, let's all get back to the road and out of this rain. Then, sir, perhaps you could take this woman away.'

Angel felt that she was perhaps not the police's favourite person.

Walking back along the ridge path to the cluster of vehicles at the car park seemed to take for ever. Mike was by her side. He said nothing but supported her when she stumbled. Now she was tired, and all she wanted was for this thing to be over. And what was Mike doing here?

Some of the police vehicles had already gone. She saw Terry being loaded into a van and managed to wave to him. Mike went to talk to Sam, then came back to join her with the superintendent.

'Well, am I under arrest, too?' she asked the superintendent.

He didn't smile. 'No, Miss Thwaite, you are not. But I'm still going to warn you. This affair has had a reasonably successful ending. It could have been an awful lot worse. The police presence was very carefully organised, with the primary aim to ensure that no one got hurt. Unlike the popular idea, we do not shoot people at random—it's the last thing we want. Eventually we would have arrested this man and I very much doubt if anyone would have been injured.'

He stopped to take a deep breath. 'You got him out and I'm very glad. But just for a minute, think of the consequences if you hadn't succeeded. Guns go off, Miss Thwaite, even when people don't really intend to shoot. How d'you think I'd feel, my men would feel—even that poor devil down there would feel—if you'd been shot? How would your relations feel? You're a nurse, Miss Thwaite. I hope you don't take these risks with your patients. Now, you'd better get home.'

'I told Martlett that I'd run you back,' Mike said. 'After all, I'm going that way.' He took her arm and led her away. She couldn't resist. Somehow she was bundled into his car, the seat belt fastened across her. Then he was driving down the hill, and the car heater slowly warmed her chilled body. She didn't have to cope any more, she could relax. Reaction set in and she burst into tears.

'Here,' he said, and handed her a handkerchief. He didn't seem very comforting and she would have liked comfort from him.

'What were you doing there?' she asked after a while.

'When I arrived, your mother said Martlett had called for you as there was trouble up on the moors. So I came up to see if I could help.' His voice suddenly grew angry. 'Then I found you were out chasing a man with a gun! Who d'you think you are? You're a nurse, not a soldier!'

'He's a friend of mine and I help who I like!'

There was a squeal of brakes as he jerked the car to the side of the road, bouncing up onto the verge. 'How d'you think I felt when

I heard what you'd done?' he yelled. Then he kissed her passionately.

She rather liked it.

'I can't cope with this,' she said when finally he released her. 'I want a hot bath and something to eat.'

'Sounds like a good idea. Your mother invited me to tea.' Then he drove on in silence again.

Something was nagging away at her, something the superintendent had said. She asked, 'You heard what that policeman said about me. I'm feeling guilty now. Well, was he right?'

'He had some good points,' Mike said judiciously. 'I thought he was a very competent and a feeling man. The trouble with you, Angel, is that when you think you're right you tend to be absolutely certain.'

'Oh,' she said, feeling rather subdued.

It was late. Her mother had sent for Nancy and they had fed Suzanne who was now sleeping. Marion said hello to Mike, kissed her daughter and said that there was a casserole in the oven but that she was going to bed.

'And I'm going to have a bath,' said Angel, and took a cup of tea in there with her. After a long soak she felt tired but much better. She could cope with whatever else the evening might bring. She put on a long robe and went back into the living room.

Mike was still there. He had laid the table and when she came in he fetched the casserole from the oven. After she had eaten she felt even better still.

'It's been an eventful evening,' he offered after a while. 'I was very concerned about you. I didn't want anything to happen to you.'

'Nothing did happen to me and now I'm fine. Thanks for your concern and in future I will try to think before I do anything hazardous.' She paused a minute and then said, 'We don't need to talk about it any more. We revert to how we were. There's no need for more talk.'

'Then it's time I was leaving.' At the door he turned and said, 'But I feel the need for talk. You might have your feelings firmly under control, Angel. I haven't. When I heard you were out on the moors, looking for a man with a gun, I…I wondered what I would do if anything happened to you.'

'Suzanne would still have been well looked after,' she said feebly.

'You know damn well that I'm not talking about Suzanne!'

Then he was gone.

CHAPTER EIGHT

OCCASIONALLY it happened. Angel was a paediatric nurse, with the 405 qualification—there were only three of them at Micklekirk Hospital. None was on duty and one was needed urgently. The phone rang at seven next morning. She listened to the message then said, 'Right, I'll be there in half an hour.' Then she phoned Nancy, to ask her to collect Suzanne earlier than expected.

The mother had been brought in the day before with a urinary tract infection. She was twenty-five weeks pregnant and a scan had shown she was having twins. And then, in spite of efforts made to stop it, it became horribly obvious that she was going to give birth—at twenty-five weeks. The twins had been born, one weighing 700 grams, one weighing 750 grams. Between them they weighed about the same as a bag of sugar. They needed ultra-specialist care, and would have to be sent to the coast when they had been stabilised.

Would Angel come and special one, and then ride with her in the ambulance? Of course she would. But it made for a hard day.

Looking after Suzanne was fun. Marion, of course, doted on her—this was the kind of work she had been trained for. Mike called every night and now they had things sorted out between them Angel quite looked forward to his visits. He would come to play with his little charge, feed her and bathe her, rock her to sleep and then perhaps have tea with them.

It happened late one night when her mother had gone to bed. Suzanne had been crying. Mike had lifted her from her cot and was walking up and down with her in his arms. Angel was sitting on the couch, watching him—and suddenly the tears were running silently down her face.

It was a while before he noticed. 'Angel, sweetheart—what is it?' He was concerned.

It took her a while before she could say what she was feeling. 'I had a baby of my own once.'

He stood motionless. '*We* had a baby,' he said.

He looked down at the now silent Suzanne, then with extra care took her out of the room to lay her in her cot. When he returned he sat on the other side of the couch, reached out and took her hand.

'We were two students living together,' he said, 'both studying, both working like fury, both dedicated. The little spare time we had we spent together. And...did we love each other?'

'Sort of,' she said eventually. 'We were two young animals, we loved each other's bodies. It used to excite me just to see you walking towards me down the corridor, looking all sleepy and dozy-eyed.'

'Everything you did excited me. We were great together, and then we discovered you were pregnant.'

Pregnant. More than seven years ago but she could still remember how it had felt. A kind of guilty joy. It hadn't been a good time for her or Mike's career to have a baby, it would have been troublesome—but she still remembered the joy. She had felt fulfilled. At first

Mike had been shocked, but then he, too, had looked forward to being a parent.

'Both of us were a bit wild,' she said, 'a bit careless. It wasn't your fault or mine, it was both of us. We wanted each other so much that we took a risk. The number of girls I've warned against that!'

'I'll never forget that day we decided to get married. Just we two at the registry office, two friends, Mark and Penny, with us. Do you remember, Angel? A meal together in a Chinese restaurant and no time for a honeymoon. Almost as if nothing had happened.'

'I didn't even tell my parents. Dad was very ill, Ma was worried sick about him—it wouldn't have been right to worry them. And I thought that when things were easier we could have had a blessing in Laxley Parish Church and a proper party.'

'And we both worked that night.'

They stopped for a moment, memories churning through their minds.

'I lost the baby,' she said. 'At about three months. I'd barely got used to the idea of being pregnant.'

'That's what you told me,' Mike said. 'I remember coming home. You were in bed, white-faced, and you'd been crying. But you said you were OK, and I told myself I believed you. But it wasn't true, was it?'

'No! It wasn't true! I felt my life had been torn apart. And after the first time I couldn't even weep for my lost baby. I didn't want to upset you. You were working so hard!'

He looked stricken. 'You never said. I loved you, Angel, you could have leaned on me more.'

'I told myself that it was just hormonal, that in a couple of weeks the pain would go away. All I had to do was work, work like you were doing, and the pain would pass. But it didn't go away—not ever, really.'

'Is that when you started to dislike Manchester—why you wanted to go to Buxton?'

The question startled her, it was something she had never thought of. But then she said, 'Yes, I suppose it was.'

'Now I realise I never knew fully how you felt about losing the baby. Angel, I'm so sorry. But did you ever wonder how I felt?'

Another startling question. No, she had never wondered how he'd felt. She had been so wrapped up in her own misery, but trying to keep up a happy front, that she had never really thought that Mike might have been affected.

'No,' she said after a while, 'I wanted to protect myself and just kept pushing you away. You mean that…'

'I mean that I thought the best thing for you was not to show any emotion. But I certainly felt it.'

'We *did* make a mess of things, didn't we?' she said.

Other than his visits to them, Mike didn't appear to have any social life at all. He was a handsome man and many of the female staff in Micklekirk would have been delighted to go out with him. But he appeared dedicated solely to his work and his new child. Angel knew there was gossip about the pair of them, but she didn't care. The people who mattered to her knew exactly what the situation was.

'You could stay overnight if you wanted,' she said to him. 'We keep that room warm and it would be a change from your bare little place in the residency.'

'Thanks, Angel. But for the moment it's better if I sleep in hospital.'

There was tolerably good news about Terry. The two men who had jeered at him were well-known local trouble-makers—in fact, Terry had been mixed up with them before. Their Land Rover turned out to have stolen goods in the back. The witness to the affray said that Terry had been assaulted first, and the police decided that he had not fired the shotgun at their car on purpose, it had been an accident. Terry would have to serve a little more time but he felt he could take it.

Angel wrote to him and got a letter back, which she showed to Mike. 'Terry knows who his friends are,' he said.

'He'd do the same for me,' Angel replied.

About a fortnight after her evening on the moors Mike phoned her on the ward and asked if she could come up to his consulting room. 'I want this to be official,' he said, 'doctor to patient stuff.'

'Properly, I should be talking to your mother,' he said when she was sitting opposite him, 'and I will later. But I want to discuss this with you first. I've scheduled your mother's operation for next week. But I've been seeing a lot of her recently and she's become a friend. I'm still wondering if I ought to carry out the operation. We could transfer her to a larger hospital on the coast.'

'No way,' Angel said. 'I can sympathise with your point of view, but I think you're the best surgeon around and I want you to do the job. Anyway, Ma wouldn't be happy in some distant place, she wants to be here among friends.'

He thought for a minute. 'All right, then,' he said. 'Next Wednesday?'

'That's perfect. I've already arranged things with Nancy and there'll be no difficulty looking after Suzanne. She'll move into Nancy's house for a while. What time next Wednesday?'

'In the afternoon, I think. It should take quite some time. We'll have her in overnight on Tuesday, though, for the usual preps. We'll send her an official letter.'

'I'll tell her myself,' said Angel. 'She's been getting a bit restive recently. She wants to get it over with.'

That night she told her mother and then phoned her brother. Martin offered to come up on the Tuesday but she told him it wasn't necessary. 'She'll be comatose for quite a while so there'll be little point in you coming. I'll phone you with any news. But if you could get up for the weekend, that would be super.'

'I'll fly up next Friday,' he said.

Angel accompanied Marion to the hospital on Tuesday and saw her settled in. As a nurse herself, she knew how to draw the fine line between supporting her mother and getting in the way of the staff. Her mother was supremely confident, already planning her new life when she was fully fit.

'I love looking after Suzanne,' she said. 'I wouldn't mind looking after a couple more children at the same time.' She looked at Angel speculatively. 'What do you think?' she asked.

'I think you should concentrate on one thing at a time,' said Angel.

Her mother was prepped the next morning. Angel stood by the trolley, holding her hand just before Marion was to be wheeled to Theatre. Her mother smiled up at her. 'I know who he is, you know,' she said.

'Know who who is?' Angel asked, puzzled.

'Mike, of course, the man who's going to operate on me. He's your ex-husband.'

Angel looked down at her mother in horror. 'How d'you know that? Has he told you? He said that—'

'He's never said a word to me. But eight years ago, while you were training, I came over to Manchester to see you just for the day. You father was very ill and I…I needed a change. I was going to surprise you. Then I saw you in the distance with Mike, and I asked someone who it was with you. They said it was your new husband. You were so obviously happy that I decided not to talk to you, not to spoil your happiness.'

Angel's eyes filled with tears. 'Oh, Ma! You should have come over! You came all that way and then you went back? That's terrible!'

'It doesn't matter now. Then your father died and I kept on expecting you to confide in me, but you didn't. Instead, you got withdrawn and remote, and then you went to South America.'

'I thought I'd forgotten him,' said Angel. 'Mike turned up here by accident and it was a shock to us both.'

'So how d'you feel about him now?'

'Right now I don't feel anything about him. I'm only interested in getting this operation over and you back on your feet again. I'll worry about Mike when that's done.'

A nurse and a porter arrived. 'Time to go to Theatre, Mrs Thwaite.'

'Listen,' her mother said, 'I don't want you hanging around, worrying. Go and do some nursing or some shopping or something. It'll only annoy me to think of you sitting brooding here.'

'Ok, Ma, I'll do that.' She stooped to kiss the smiling face. The trolley was wheeled away.

She wasn't on duty but she went down to her ward, changed and generally made herself useful. She had arranged that when the operation was over she would be contacted, but three hours and then four passed so she phoned the ward. Mrs Thwaite wasn't back from Theatre yet.

Still in her uniform, Angel crossed over to the cardiac centre. The theatre doors were still closed so the operation was presumably still be in progress. She went round the back to where there was a viewing gallery. A handful of medical students were watching intently. Angel kept her eyes from the brightly illuminated figure in the centre. She sat next to a student. 'How're things going?' she asked.

'Fantastic! It started off as a routine valve replacement for a mitral stenosis, then the patient arrested and there were all sorts of complications. That lady there should have died, but this fellow Gilmour wouldn't let her go. He tried everything and I guess he succeeded. She might still make it, but I'm not sure.'

'Now I have to repair this vein insertion. Notice how little room there is for manoeuvre. You never move fast here.' Suddenly Mike's voice echoed round the gallery. Angel remembered that surgeons could give a commentary to help anyone who might be watching. It made things even more unreal.

She became aware that the student was talking to her, his voice concerned. 'Are you all right, love? Put your head between your legs and I'll fetch you a glass of water. We don't expect nurses to faint, do we?'

'That's my mother being operated on,' she said.

The student was young but in time he'd be a good doctor. He put his arm round her, lifted her bodily. 'Come on, out, this is no place for you.'

'No. I mean, I want to—'

'You can tell me outside.' She was half helped, half dragged out of the viewing gallery.

He found her somewhere to sit and fetched her a drink. 'Look,' he said, 'I'm sorry for what I said but, with you being in uniform, I thought you were just a nurse with an interest.'

'That's all right. I'll stay here now. Will you come and tell me how she's...how things are going?'

She could even admire the casual good nature of the man. 'Of course I will. I'll be back to see you at intervals. Now, can I get you another coffee?'

In fact, he came to see her three times. 'I would say she's well out of danger now,' he said after the second visit, 'bearing in mind that things can always go wrong. But that was a brilliant bit of surgery.' Later he came to say that things were over. The operation had been a success.

Her mother was in the recovery room and because Angel was a nurse she was allowed in. She had seen people after operations before and was expecting how her mother would look, so pale as to be almost grey, with a sense of the entire body being diminished. But she was going to survive.

Then she went looking for Mike. His greens were covered in blood. 'I want to change before I talk to you,' he muttered. 'Things were harder than I had expected but she should be all right now.'

'I know it was harder. I was up in the gallery.'

'You were what?'

'It was OK. A student took me out.' She looked at him. He was swaying slightly, and grey with fatigue. 'You look terrible,' she said.

'It's nothing to what I'm feeling,' he said honestly, 'but the job is done and I'm glad.'

'Have your shower, get changed, then come back to the bungalow and sleep there. You can bring your mobile with you. If you're needed you can get back.'

'I'm very tempted. But why are you inviting me?'

'Because I want you there. I need you there. I don't want to be on my own tonight. Because you're dead on your feet and I don't want you to go to your impersonal little hospital room. Let someone else look after you for a while.'

'Angel, I'm all right!'

'No, you're not. You look terrible. Any minute now you're going to fall down.'

'Well, the last time I came back to your place feeling like this I—'

'Whatever,' she said. 'You seemed to be happy enough.'

Mike was still very tired but she could see him coming round, see the spark of intelligence alight in his eyes again. 'One thing,' he said. 'No, two things. First, I don't want simple gratitude, I'm a well-paid surgeon. Second, whatever this night brings, afterwards we talk. I don't feel like being silent any more.'

It only took her a moment to decide. 'Fine,' she said. 'If you want to talk then we'll talk. I've been frightened of it but I know we'll have to. See you back at the bungalow.'

She went to see her mother again, though she knew there was little point. The nurse in charge knew her, and after five minutes chased her away. 'You know there's nothing you can do! If we need to, we'll be in touch.'

So she phoned her brother, who had said he wanted her to get in touch at any time. 'It took a little longer than we expected, Martin. But Mike thinks she should be all right.'

'That makes me feel easier. I like that guy and I've got a lot of confidence in him. See you on Friday!'

She went home, undressed and showered. The clothes she was wearing seemed sticky, though they had all been fresh on that morning. It was as if emotion had seeped out of her very skin. She changed into a tracksuit.

Mike arrived ten minutes later. He, too, was freshly showered, and was dressed in jeans and sweater. But there were still dark marks under his eyes and he seemed to move more slowly than usual.

She made him tea, and then served him the soup her mother made in large quantities. Good stock, a variety of vegetables, a thickening of green lentils and a selection of herbs and spices that was a family secret. When he had eaten he looked less fatigued. She took him to the sitting room and sat beside him on the couch.

'Just before the anaesthetist did his bit I had a word with Marion,' he said. 'She winked at me and said, "I've got every confidence in you, son." Have you told her about us?'

Angel said, 'She knows we were married but I didn't tell her. Apparently she came to Manchester one day and saw us together.'

He looked at her, amazed. 'And she never said anything to you?'

'No. She knew that if there was any reason to tell her anything I would do so. But there wasn't.'

'No, there wasn't,' he said bleakly. Then he frowned. 'Why has your mother chosen this time to confide in both of us? It seems odd.'

'I've no idea,' Angel said, 'but you can bet there is a reason.'

For a while both of them thought about this. Then he said, 'Your mother is a truly remarkable woman. You know I never knew my own mother. If I had, I hope she'd have been like yours.'

'That's a true compliment,' she said quietly.

There was another short silence and then Mike said, 'Look, I've got work tomorrow. I just have to go to bed.'

This was it. She knew after the last time she couldn't hope for or expect help from him. Steeling herself, she said, 'D'you want me to come with you?'

'You know I do, Angel! But why do you ask me? What d'you want? Last time was…well, better than anything that has ever happened to me in my life. And then your letter was so stark. I could sympathise, of course. With what we'd both been through before, I didn't want that again.'

'Nor me,' Angel said. She laughed nervously. 'Mike, are you asking me to persuade you to get into my bed?'

'You never used to have to do that, did you?' he asked, and she blushed. He went on, 'I'll answer your question. I want you now. I wonder if I ever really stopped loving you. Now I want you desperately, but not just for tonight and with no future. I want your promise that we talk some time, and your promise that we go out together all of this coming Sunday.'

'Go out where?' she asked curiously.

'I want to keep that a secret. But I think you'll be interested.'

'All right, then, so long as Ma is OK.'

'She will be,' he promised.

'Right. Decision time. Mike, will you go and get in my bed and I'll be with you in five minutes? I just can't go and leave the washing-up.'

'Just like that? Get up and walk to your bed?'

'If it's hard then I'll take you.' She stood in front of him, pulled him to his feet. Then she kissed him, softly, gently, a kiss with the promise of good things to come. Slipping an arm round his waist, she urged him towards the door. In her bedroom she lit the bedside lamp, slid her nightie from under the pillow. 'Five minutes,' she whispered.

'After six minutes I'll be asleep.'

Angel needed that short time to herself. The washing-up was done practically at once, and then she went to the bathroom to clean her teeth. She undressed and looked at herself naked in the full-length mirror. She was twenty-eight. Her waist was as trim, her breasts as firm and high as they had been when she was eighteen. She picked up her nightie, then put it down again. It wouldn't be needed.

She wasn't sure where this would lead, why she was doing it or what it would mean to her. She only knew that she wanted it—needed it—more desperately than anything she had needed in years.

Naked, she went to her bedroom. With only the bedside lamp on, it was in half-darkness. Mike was lying there, obviously naked himself but with a sheet drawn up to his waist. As she looked at him his expression was unreadable. He was tired but there was a glimmer in his eyes that said that he was as interested in her as she was in him.

She slid under the sheet and for a while they were content just to lie there, hands gently stroking each other's bodies. Both were weary, and she felt something infinitely comforting in the way he touched her. His hands strayed across her shoulders, lovingly caressed the slopes and peaks of her breasts, squeezed her waist and then trailed downwards. She sighed, then gasped. Suddenly she wasn't tired any more.

His body felt electric beneath her touch, she wondered at the effect even the least little contact could have on him. She smiled to herself, did it again.

'If you carry on doing that,' he panted, 'if you don't stop doing that...' So she did it even more.

'Do it like this, you mean?' she asked. 'What will you do, Mike, if I do it like this?'

For someone so fatigued he could move remarkably quickly. One moment they were side by side, smiling, kissing, touching gently. And then he pushed her down, stretched across her naked body and was poised above her. For a moment she felt almost afraid, but... 'I want you Mike,' she muttered.

She wrapped her arms round him, pulled him to her, into her, for this was something they should do together. For her then there was only the desperate urge to a swift and longed-for climax.

She kissed him softly on the lips. 'You can sleep now,' she said.

'You'll be by me in the morning?' Even though he was so tired she could hear the anxiety in his voice.

'Oh, yes, my love,' she promised. Within seconds he was asleep.

Once again Angel woke early. Mike was fast asleep, there was no way he would wake on his own. Just to be wicked she leaned over and kissed him lightly on the lips. He didn't even move. She looked down at him. His face was now relaxed, more youthful-looking in sleep. In the past she had often done this. Of the two of them, he was the heaviest sleeper. She felt a great surge of—it was love.

Trying not to disturb him, she crept out of bed, put on the kettle and then phoned her mother's ward. Marion had had a good night. She was still very tired but her condition was fine. Angel should visit her later in the day when she would be better able to talk.

A sleepy voice came from her bedroom. 'Do I hear the sound of a kettle boiling?'

'Stay in that bed,' she shouted back. 'There's at least an hour before you need to leave for the hospital.'

'Talked me into it.'

She took two mugs of tea to the bedroom, slid again in beside him. 'Before anything,' she ordered, 'especially before talking, you drink your tea. You make more sense when you've woken up.'

'Whatever you say, miss.' He pulled himself up in bed and she reached over to drop a pillow behind his head. As she did so he leaned forward and kissed her breast.

'Mike! Tea first, I told you.' Firmly, she placed the mug in his hand.

They drank in contented silence, again aware of naked legs, hips, shoulders, just touching. It was gently arousing.

'Last night I was tired,' he said sleepily. 'I felt my manhood was under attack. I need to reassert myself in a very positive manner.'

'Your manhood seemed to be as certain as my womanhood,' she told him, 'but what did you have in mind? Oh. I see.' Her body arched in ecstasy.

This time their love-making took longer, was more inventive, finished in a joint climax that seemed to throb inside her and go on and on and on. For ten minutes they lay there, content just to hold each other. Then she decided to be practical.

'We have five minutes for a bacon sandwich each,' she said. 'That'll be a pleasure of an entirely different kind.'

'Being with you is always so exciting and so different,' he said. 'What else can we do?'

'We can go to work. Mike, last time I think we took things in too much of a hurry. Don't worry, I'm not going to leave you another note. But I want us to go carefully, to decide what we can give each other, as well as what we want. If we're to have any kind of relationship I want it to be one that will last. Don't you agree?' Her voice was pleading.

'Yes, I do,' he said. 'That is, I suppose I do. This time work isn't going to get in the way of what we have for each other. Tonight I'm on call and tomorrow I'm off to run a clinic at that place further south for the day. When did you say Martin was coming up?'

'Tomorrow. He'll stay overnight, visit Ma and go back late Saturday. And I'm not having noisy sex with you if he's in the spare bedroom.'

'Pity. I'd like to see him, though. And remember you're spending Sunday with me. It'll be a sort of test.'

She was curious. 'A test? What sort of test?'

'One that I think you'll enjoy. Wear something nice and feminine—we're not going for a walk. Oh, and bring a hat.'

'A hat! What will I do with a hat? Mike, where are you taking me? I want to know!'

He grinned. 'I love teasing you when you're stark naked,' he said. 'Somehow it makes everything different.'

CHAPTER NINE

MIKE said Angel should visit Marion after he had seen her. He would be making a routine visit to check up on her progress at about eleven. So she waited till he had been in the ward and talked to him afterwards.

'Nothing to report,' he said, 'which is good. As you know, it was a serious operation and there were complications. But everything is as it should be now. I see no reason why she shouldn't make a complete recovery and have a much enhanced lifestyle afterwards.'

'You just want her to look after Suzanne,' Angel grumbled.

'And look after me a bit,' he said urbanely. 'I could live on that family soup that she made.'

Angel was a nurse and she knew better than to be intimidated by the battery of instruments that monitored her mother's progress. Most of them she used herself with her neonates. But it was different when your mother was the patient.

Marion was awake, but still drugged. Angel sat with her for a while, held her hand and thought she saw a spark of recognition when her mother's eyes slowly opened. Then she had a quick word with the nurse and went to her own ward. Everything was going well. It would take time, of course, but everything was going well.

She felt the prick of tears in her eyes and had to stop and run into a cloakroom. It was relief, of course, but only now did she understand what kind of a strain she had been under. Now was a time for celebration! Well, it would be in a week or two.

Martin had sent her strict instructions for his arrival on Friday. He was not to be met and again he would hire a car at the airport. He would go straight to the hospital to see their mother and then come to the bungalow. Angel considered for a minute, and then invited Mike to join them for a meal that evening. She knew the two men got on well.

Mike arrived early, carrying a bottle of wine. She let him in, snatched a kiss, then sent him into the living room. 'Go and chat to Martin,' she said. 'I'm going to be another hour doing exciting things in the kitchen and I don't want to be disturbed.'

A couple of minutes after he'd gone into the room there was a burst of laughter, and then her brother put his head round the kitchen door. 'If you're doing wonderful things in here for a while, us two men are going to the pub for half an hour.'

'If you do then you wash up!'

'We were expecting to do that anyway. Be back in time for tea!' And they were gone.

She was pleased that the two got on so well. But then she wondered if they would talk about her. Her brother was a shrewd business-man, she knew it wasn't easy to fool him. If he asked Mike what his relationship was with her, what would Mike say? She shrugged. Nothing she could do about it now.

It was a good meal and the three of them had a pleasant evening together. Mike left quite early, saying he had some work to do before the next day. Martin, too, was ready for an early night as the travelling had tired him. Angel sat up in bed, thinking about what had passed. Yes, it had been a good evening—casual but interesting. She couldn't remember the last time she had sat down to a meal with two men.

When Angel and Martin went to see her next day, their mother was much better, sitting up in bed and talking about the future. They arranged that when she was discharged she would go to stay with Martin for a further fortnight.

My life's taken a new track, Angel thought as they walked down the corridor. I knew Ma would have to have her operation, and I knew we'd have to leave High Walls, but I hadn't expected half the excitement that I've had. And all due to Mike. My ex-husband, the man I'd almost forgotten.

No, you hadn't, an honest little voice told her.

She was sorry that Martin had to go back so soon. But he had enjoyed his trip, he said, and he was much happier now he'd seen his mother. 'I'm glad to see I'm leaving the family in such good hands,' he said. She wondered what exactly he meant by that.

When Martin had gone Angel phoned Mike and boldly asked him if he'd like to come to stay the night.

'You know how much I want to stay,' he said, 'but I'm not going to. First reason—I'm on call and I've got a very good idea I'm going to be hauled out of my bed at least twice. Second reason—we still have to talk. I don't want to spoil what we've got again, Angel.'

'1 suppose you're right,' she said gloomily. Then she brightened up. They were to spend all the next day together. 'Tell me about this hat I've got to wear tomorrow. And won't you give me just a hint as to where we're going?'

'We-e-ell—no. But make the hat a frivolous one, and I will tell you we'll spend some time in church. Another thing, we're going to be in the car for quite a while, so if you want to travel in something comfortable and then change in a pub or something, that'll be fine.'

Stranger and stranger. But he wouldn't tell her where they were going, only that she'd find it interesting.

She picked a light blue dress that went well with her blonde hair, and matched it with a darker blue hat with a golden ribbon round it.

Both were draped in a polythene cover and she dressed in her normal sweater and jeans.

She spent a couple of hours round at Nancy's, helping her with a very contented Suzanne, and then came home to go to bed early, but not to sleep. She was intrigued. What *would* tomorrow bring?

As promised, Mike picked her up early next day. He was wearing a sweater over the top of a white shirt and dark trousers. The jacket and tie hung behind him. They set off at once, and for the first hour or so she was content to enjoy the drive and be with him. But then her curiosity got the better of her. 'Come on,' she said, 'you've tantalised me long enough. Where are we going and why?'

She thought he seemed a little uncertain. He paused before he answered. 'We're going to a christening,' he said. 'I'm going to be a godfather again. There will be a little party afterwards.'

Now she felt uneasy. 'A party for your friends, obviously,' she said. 'Which friends are they?'

He spoke slowly, as if each word were carefully considered. 'We're going to Manchester.

Where we first met, where we first trained and worked. We're going to the christening of Jennifer Joanne Haliwell. Mark and Penny Haliwell's third child.'

Angel sat there, unable to speak. Mark and Penny were doctors, once friends of theirs. They had been the couple who had witnessed their wedding and had shared the Chinese meal afterwards. Shortly after the wedding they had left for posts in the South and she had seen or heard nothing of them since. They had trained with Mike and had been his friends, rather than hers.

She didn't know what to say. She wasn't sure what she felt. Now she realised why Mike hadn't told her where they were going, he'd known she wouldn't have consented. This shifted the way she was beginning to think about him, to feel about him. She had been thrown back into a time she had tried to forget, tried to put behind her.

It was hard to recognise her own voice when she finally did speak. 'Will there be anyone else there that I used to know? Any more old friends?'

He shrugged. 'There might well be. Mike and Penny came straight back to Manchester after they'd finished a tour down south. They kept up with a lot of people we used to know.'

A vast anger was building up inside her. 'Mike! Stop this car! Stop it now! I want to get out. How could you do this to me?' I said *stop*!'

Fortunately there was a lay-by handy. He pulled into it and she scrabbled at the door-handle. 'Unlock this door! Unlock it now!'

Flatly, he said, 'There's a bench over there. Go and sit on it and get your breath back. When you're ready, come back and we can talk. If you want we'll turn round and I'll take you straight back home, and not say another word, I promise.'

'Just shut up! I need to be away from you.' She scrambled out of the car, walked up and down the lay-by, taking deep breaths. Her heart was pounding. Taking out her handkerchief, she wiped away tears, tears of anger not of suffering. How could he do this to her?

After a while she tired of walking and sat on the bench, looked up at the blue sky. She could hear the cry of birds, the hum of traffic on the road behind her. And slowly she calmed down. She couldn't remain angry for too long. But a deep determination grew inside her.

She walked back to the car, sat in the front without looking at him. 'You said we could talk?'

'We can talk, Angel, we have to! I knew this would be a bit of a shock for you—but I think it's for the best.'

'*You* think it's for the best. But there's two of us here. I'd almost forgotten your habit of making decisions and just expecting me to go along with them. Have you learned nothing?'

The stone face he had presented so far now looked worried. 'I thought things between us were moving. I wanted us to see together how things might have been if…perhaps I'd acted differently.'

'You, be different? Mike, couples take decisions together. It's not just you deciding what is best. I might think differently.'

He sighed. 'I'm sorry, Angel, I know you're right. But would you have come if I'd told you?'

'Probably not. Not yet. In a month or two, perhaps.'

'I suppose that's fair enough. Right, if you want I'll turn round and take you back. It's entirely your decision, and I shan't say a word.'

She couldn't bring herself to say it. For a while she was silent and then she said, 'Tell me about Mark and Penny.'

'I've kept in touch with them for years. They've both done rather well. He's a senior registrar in Manchester and she's done a variety of locum jobs while bringing up the kids.'

'Did you tell them I was coming with you?'

'Yes. They're both looking forward to seeing you. We'll call at the house first for a quick bite, then there's the church service and then back in the afternoon for a little party.'

She guessed that didn't sound too bad. Besides, she was curious. 'All right,' she said, 'let's go. I'd like to see them—I think. Do they know what our situation is?'

He said nothing but his relief was obvious. 'They know we've just met again by accident. Don't worry, they won't say anything that might be unfortunate.'

'Doesn't leave much to talk about, does it?'

Most of the rest of the journey took place in silence. When they got nearer Manchester they stopped at a motorway café and had coffee, then she went to change into her navy dress. Once in the car she put her hat on.

'Am I allowed to say I think you look absolutely gorgeous in that?' he asked.

'Don't push your luck, Gilmour. I have neither forgotten not forgiven.'

Once they came off the motorway and started to drive through the suburbs, she felt a little restless. 'Where do they live?' she asked.

'Rather a pleasant district on the east side. You can see the Pennines from their back garden.'

'Anywhere near where we used to live?'

It was a while before he replied. Then he said, 'Their house would be about twenty minutes' drive from Grove Street. Do you want to pass there? We're in plenty of time.'

Did she want to see where she had lived? And if so, why? She just didn't know. Now she was edgy. 'No,' she said… 'That is, I don't know, it was only a flat. But there again…yes, I want to see it again.'

Angel's mood became even more uncertain as she started to pass landmarks she recognised, places she had visited. 'I've not been to Manchester since we split up,' she said abruptly. 'I guess I've avoided it.'

'I've done the same,' Mike said laconically, 'and, anyway, they say you can never go back.'

Finally they drove down the High Street. This district of Seaton had once been a small town of its own. It had been swallowed up by Manchester but still seemed to be a community of its own. And she found that the memories that returned were all happy.

'There's the chippy we used to go to,' she shouted. 'Remember the James's Special? We used to get extra pork because the owner's daughter had been very well treated in hospital. And we went in that pub…and that one… Remember how we used to play darts?'

'I remember very well,' he said.

On an area of waste ground a gigantic new supermarket had been built, open twenty-four hours a day. 'We could have done with that,' he said. 'Remember the number of times we needed something to eat and there was nowhere open?'

'We used to keep emergency supplies of beans and crisp breads. Beans and crisp breads! What a diet!'

'I can think of far worse meals,' he said.

He looked at the passing pedestrians. 'I think this is still the same kind of district,' he said. 'It has the same feel to it. Look, I'll swear that bunch are medical students!'

'They have that look. They all have that superior look that they teach in medical school.'

'Angel! I said I was sorry.'

He turned right into a short cul-de-sac. There on their right it was. Number 2 Grove Street, part of a short terrace of three-storey houses. Angel looked up at the first-floor flat where she had lived with Mike. That was their living room with windows on two walls, that was their bedroom that only got the sun last thing at night on summer days. But the curtains had always been shut anyway…

'I've had enough of this,' she said sharply. 'Those times are gone. We're not students now, neither of us are.'

'I agree. But don't you want to get out and walk round for a while?'

'No. I have a new life now. I don't want to waste time looking back at an old one.'

He drove on then, and neither of them spoke. She thought he was as affected by memories as she was. There was a bitter-sweet sense of what had been, of what had happened and of what might have happened. She realised that there was so much she had forgotten, probably deliberately. Going back was dangerous.

She was glad when they entered a hilly, leafy suburb. If you had to live in a town, this would be the place. They turned into the drive of a detached house and now she felt nervous in a different way. What would her welcome be? Mike had said that Mark and Penny were looking forward to seeing her. Why should they?

'Uncle Mike, Uncle Mike!' Two little girls came running out, aged about five, one in a long pink dress, the other in a long blue dress. Obviously they were twins.

Mike jumped out of the car, picked one up in each arm and swung them round. 'How's my two little girlfriends? I want a kiss from each of you.' Solemnly they each leaned forward and kissed him. It was easy to see that he was a favourite.

Angel got slowly out of the car, holding her hat in her hand. She was aware of two sets of eyes looking at her steadily. Mike said, 'Samantha and Sarah, I want you to meet Angel. She's a very special friend of mine and she's helping me look after a little girl.'

After a moment, either Samantha or Sarah said, 'She can't be an angel. Angels have long white dresses on, and wings.'

The other Sarah or Samantha said, with the air of one trying to be fair, 'But she's got the right colour hair, hasn't she?'

Angel bent down and said, 'I'm sorry I'm not a real angel. But first can you tell me which of you is Sarah and which is Samantha? And then can I have a kiss anyhow?'

She was duly kissed by Sarah—in pink—and Samantha—in blue. Then a voice behind her said, 'And can I have a kiss, too? I'd recognise that lovely hair anywhere.'

She turned, and there was Mark. He was a bit older, a bit fatter, had lost a little hair. But there was that cheerful expression she remembered so well, and that genuine pleasure to see her. She put her arms round him, and as he hugged her she discovered that that was just what she wanted. She hugged him back hard. This was how it always had been. 'Angel, it's been far, far too long,' he said, and she had to agree.

She had missed Mark, had missed the rest of the friends she had shared with Mike. She had given them up, if not willingly then with determination. They had been a part of her life that had ended. She had cut it out ruthlessly, and now she found herself wishing she hadn't.

She turned to see Penny in an apron, smiling at her. I want to be kissed, too,' she said. 'Then both of you come in for a while before lunch.'

There were just a couple of relations for lunch, and Angel was introduced as an old friend. Then she put on her hat, went to church and enjoyed the service and christening. She couldn't help comparing the happiness and the ease with the last christening she had been to—when she and Mike had become godparents to a child that both had thought would die.

Afterwards there was a party at the house. Angel played with the twins, talked with Penny, thoroughly enjoyed herself. In fact, she didn't see too much of Mike—he seemed to be monopolised by some important people from Mark's hospital. But from time to time she was aware of him looking at her.

Eventually they had a moment together. 'Why are you looking at me as if you're worried?' she asked. 'Every time I look up you seem gloomy, and I'm having a wonderful time.'

Soberly he said, 'I really am pleased you're enjoying yourself. I'm very pleased. But bringing you here was a gamble, and I'm still worried about it not coming off.' He glanced at the two dark-suited older men who had been talking to him so seriously. 'And things aren't being helped by people who are determined to talk shop.'

'Ah, well, that's your fault for becoming so important. But if you're worried about your gamble, then I should stop. I think you've won. I'm having a super time.'

'Things aren't over yet. You promised me we could have a talk soon. How will coming here affect us, d'you think?'

'I can guess what you want to talk about. I want to talk, too, but I'm afraid that when we do things will be clearer that I want kept in the dark. But I do agree that coming here has made things a bit more complex. If nothing else, it has made me rethink things I once was certain about. And I'm not sure I like that.'

'All I want is to—' But then they were disturbed again and she never found out what was troubling him.

Eventually most of the guests disappeared. The twins sat and watched a video and there were only Mark and Mike, Penny and herself sitting holding cups of tea. Mark and Mike were now talking shop. 'I've been working towards this for years,' Mike was saying. 'I've had the training in America. I can start in London and introduce a whole new programme.'

'When d'you expect to start?'

'As soon as I can. I'm very happy in Micklekirk—there's a great team there and it's one of the best run hospitals I've ever seen. But I need to get back into the heart of things. I'm going to buy a flat in the centre of

London—you'll have to come down and visit, stay with me and Suzanne.'

'Look forward to it,' said Mark. 'We like the occasional visit to the capital.'

Angel drank her tea and considered. She knew this already, but she'd had a tiny hope that perhaps, just perhaps, Mike might have thought again. After all, he was back in her life again. Mike and Suzanne—her temporary family…

So he was still going to buy a central flat in London. Where did that leave her? Was he going to invite her to live with him—so far away? Could she to go with him? Might she be falling in love again, or was it just a case of realising her feelings for him had never truly died?

One thing was certain. Before she did anything she had to be sure she wasn't on the same destructive course as she had embarked on before.

'It's been so lovely seeing you again,' Penny said, just before she and Mike left. 'We always thought of you as our friend, you know, not just…not just…'

'Not just Mike's wife,' Angel finished cheerfully. 'Don't worry, now I know where you are I'll be here again, either with him or not. You've no idea how much I've enjoyed being here. Bye, Penny.'

After a shaky start it had been a good day. And now there was so much to think about. 'If you don't mind,' she said as they drove back, 'I want to postpone this serious talk we're going to have. I don't want to have it now, I don't even want to have it tonight. I need at least one night's sleep to get my mind round what's happened today. It's altered no end of things.'

'Altered things—or brought them back?'

'That's what I want to consider,' she said firmly. 'Now, leave it till tomorrow night. I want to decide if I've been deceiving myself for the past seven years. Mike, it's very easy to believe that you're right and all the rest of the world is wrong.'

'Don't I know it. All right, Angel, I'm quite happy to wait. You've got to feel comfortable.'

'Just one thing, though. I want you to stay at the bungalow tonight. If you want to, that is.'

'Oh, I do. I most definitely do. Especially if you cook me some more of that wonder soup that your family makes.'

'Is that the only reason you want to stay?'

'What other reason could there possibly be?' he asked.

They called at the hospital. Mike needed to check on one or two appointments. She went to see her mother and found her almost her old self. 'Nancy brought Suzanne in to see me. I think that little darling has grown since I saw her last. She looks a really healthy baby now, Angel. How have you spent the day?'

'I've been to Manchester with Mike. We saw some old friends of ours.'

'Ah,' said her mother. 'Well, don't tell me all the details now, I'm still a bit tired. But when you're ready—and if you want—I'd like to hear everything.'

Angel leaned forward to kiss her mother. 'You're one in a million,' she said.

She made Mike the soup he wanted when they got to the bungalow, but the evening was still early. 'There's a play I really want to see on TV,' she told him. 'D'you want to sit and watch with me? It's an adaptation of a nineteenth-century novel.'

'A play! I haven't watched a play on TV in years!'

'Then this is a good time to start. You can sit by me and read the paper if you like. We'll be together and I think we need a bit of time when all we do is just sit with each other.'

He put his arm round her, kissed her gently on the forehead. 'That's a nice idea. You watch, I'll read.'

So they sat side by side on the couch, mugs of tea in front of them. She thought it was a good adaptation—the clothes, settings, even language gave the feeling of the times. But the emotions were so easy to recognise. Love was universal.

At first he merely glanced at the screen occasionally, reading the paper most of the time. But then she saw him become more and more interested, more and more intent. The paper was dropped and ignored. When she reached for and held his hand, he squeezed it almost abstractedly.

When the play was finished she sighed with delight and said, 'It's lovely, watching with you. I feel so relaxed, so…well…togetherish.'

'Togetherish it is,' he agreed. 'Now, it's not very late, but shall we go to bed?'

This time she bathed and got into bed first. It was quietly arousing, lying there, waiting for him. He came into the bedroom with only a towel wrapped round him and knelt on the bed by her side.

'I know what we're going to do now,' he said, 'and it will be wonderful. But I want to say something first. And I don't want you to say anything back because you might feel obliged. I love you, Angel.'

She looked at him, wide-eyed. When she opened her mouth he gently put his hand over it. 'No more talk now,' he said. 'We can talk tomorrow. Just remember, I do love you, Angel.'

Then he slid into the bed by her side and this time their love-making was more explosive than ever before.

They were early to bed again the following night. But this was to be a serious meeting. To emphasise this fact, Angel had put on a nightie, one she called her Wee-Willie-Winkie nightie, long-sleeved, high-necked, in thick pink material.

'It doesn't work. I'm afraid you look sexier than ever,' he told her glumly.

At hospital she had told him that if he was going to stay the night, he had to bring pyjamas. 'For the first hour anyway,' she said.

He'd looked panic-stricken. 'I haven't got any pyjamas,' he said. 'Shall I wear a long shirt?'

'If that's the best you can do.'

But this was to be a serious meeting, and she knew as he sat upright in bed beside her that he would treat it seriously. This was the talk he had asked for. 'You asked for this—you start,' she told him. In truth, she wasn't sure what she would say herself.

It seemed hard for him to start. 'I feel we should be at the Drovers' Arms,' he told her, 'where we've had our other heart-to-heart talks.'

She giggled. 'You couldn't dress like that in the Drovers'. This is a good place to negotiate. Neither of us will get angry, we can each see what there is to lose.' Then she grew serious. 'When we were married we didn't talk enough,' she said. 'We just kept on being happy, working and hoping that things would sort themselves out. And they didn't. So this time we get a clear idea of each other's point of view. OK? Then it's you first.'

Mike stared at the bedroom wall opposite the bed, and his voice changed to being reflective. 'I told you last night, I love you. I think I always have. Over the past few years I've had a couple of affairs, neither of which was really serious because I just couldn't get involved. I hope no one got hurt—certainly I tried to part as gently as possible. And I always had my work. Then seeing you again was a terrific shock. I never expected to run into you again. I deliberately tried not to think of you. Now I want you more than ever but I'm not going to rush into…'

'Marriage?' she asked softly when he hesitated.

'Yes, marriage. There's a lot we have to sort out first, a lot of problems. Suzanne for a start.'

'Suzanne isn't a problem,' said Angel. 'She's a baby and she's lovely. We'll make a good life for her.'

'Good. Now it's your turn. You tell me what you feel, what you want in the future.'

There was no problem as to what came first. 'Well, I love you, too. I thought I didn't. I've spent seven years deliberately trying to forget you, but it just hasn't worked. I even tried to fight against it when you came back, but it did no good.' She pondered a moment. 'I've not had any actual affairs. I've been out with the odd man, but that's all. I was wary, I suppose. I didn't want to get into anything I couldn't handle.'

'So do we have a problem now?'

This was the heart of the matter. 'Yes, we do, a big problem. I heard you talking to Mark and you've made no secret of your ambitions—you're going to work in central London. It's a job you've always wanted and you'll be good at it. But I'm settled here. This is my life, I'm part of a community. There's no way I could live in the centre of a big town. I've done it and I hated it. So what do we do?'

He had changed in the past seven years. Once he would have instantly insisted that she give way. Now he could see her point of view, was willing to think about it. He reached over, ran his hand down her arm. Not a sexual gesture, a reassuring one.

'The first thing we do is remember that there's no need for a quick decision. I've got months of work left here in Micklekirk. We can think about things, take our time. This time we'll get things right, we'll talk them through.'

He leaned over again and this time he kissed her. 'Here's a suggestion. I'm going down to London next weekend. Come with me. Fly down Friday, come back Sunday. You can look at the hospital I'm going to work at, I'll show you the area I want to live in. Incidentally, once I tell people what you are, you'll be offered a job at once! Meet a couple of my friends, get an idea of the kind of life I'll be leading. All you have to do is look—there'll be no pressure. Think of it as a little holiday.'

It didn't take Angel long to consider. 'I'd love to come,' she said.

Marion was doing very well. She was making the most of her stay in hospital. Even Angel was surprised at the number of people she knew, the casual visitors who just turned up.

'You're an item of juicy gossip,' she cheerfully told Angel the next day. 'Everyone's got you paired off with Mike. They know about the arrangements for Suzanne and that's a good thing, but they think that now he'd better marry you.'

Angel sighed. Could anything stop hospital talk? 'What do you say?' she asked.

'I just smile sweetly and say I'm sure that everything will turn out all right in the end. I'm afraid I've irritated no end of people by not having any little titbits to tell them.'

Angel remembered that not once in seven years had her mother mentioned that she'd known her daughter had been married. This was a woman who would only say what she wanted to.

'Why did you never ask me about being married?' she asked. 'You must have wanted to know.'

'Well, I did. But it was your story, dear, and if you'd wanted to tell me you would have done. And lately I thought you'd got it beaten. Did Mike come looking for you?'

'No. This is the frightening thing. It was a complete coincidence, him coming to

Micklekirk. We might never have met again in our lives.'

Marion took one of the oranges Angel had brought her and started to peel it. 'Coincidences happen, of course. Perhaps Mike believes that coming here was a coincidence. But I'm sure you must have mentioned to him where you were born. Then he was looking for a job, just for a few months, and...perhaps he put the two ideas together without realising it.'

'You mean he subconsciously wanted to come here? He wanted to find me?'

'Yes,' Marion said with a smile. 'But don't tell him I said so. He thinks he's master of his own destiny.'

'Isn't that what we all think?' asked Angel. Could her mother be right?

'Just let me know what you think I ought to know,' her mother went on. 'I know you, you'll go your own way. You've got the strength to stand up for yourself. When you were younger I never had to worry about you the way I had to worry about Martin.'

'Thanks, Ma,' said Angel.

She was looking forward to her trip to London, she hadn't been there for quite a while. It was fun packing her bag, deciding which clothes to take, wondering what they would do when they got there. Then Friday came. Mike drove them to the airport where they had dinner, a quick flight down and then coach and taxi. It seemed to take no time at all.

He'd booked them into a hotel—a double, she had insisted. They went to their room to freshen up and then he said they'd go for a walk round, just for an hour. 'Get the feel of the place,' he said. 'You do that best by walking.'

The first thing she noticed was how hilly it was. Streets seem to climb in every direction—she liked it. She didn't like flat country.

'This is called Crouch End,' he told her. 'It's about ten minutes from the M1 and the A1M, and in the other direction a short bus journey and six stops on the underground to central London. But there's still a village atmosphere here.'

'Show me,' she said.

They went to a pub on a main road first. It was large, seemed pleasant enough and wasn't too crowded. There was a large selection of beers on offer and a chalked menu—it didn't seem too different from her own local.

Mike had a beer and bought her a red wine. She sipped, looked round and choked on her drink. She nudged him. 'Mike! Look there in the corner!' she whispered excitedly. 'That man's on TV! He's an actor in that police serial.'

Mike glanced over. 'So he is,' he said. 'Quite a lot of TV people live round here. It's pleasant but it's central, too. Don't look now, but there are three girls sitting together behind you. The one at the end is a children's programme presenter.'

When she had a chance she looked round. Yes, there she was. Smaller than Angel had thought, and not looking much out of the ordinary.

'You notice no one's staring at her,' Mike said, 'not like they would in the Cat and Fiddle in Laxley.'

'They wouldn't stare in Laxley,' she said. 'They'd look but they wouldn't stare.'

After a thoughtful pause, he said, 'You're right. They wouldn't stare.'

'Mike! I thought I'd find you here! And with a lady, too!'

Angel looked up to see a rotund looking man in a black cableknit sweater smiling cheerfully down at them. It was odd, but she liked him at once. He seemed to radiate good humour, as if he found the world, on the whole, a pretty good place to be.

'Tim, come and join us. Meet my friend Angel Thwaite—she's a trained neonatal children's nurse with midwife training and has her 405 certificate. She's vaguely, thinking—just vaguely mind you—of moving down here in a month or two. Angel, this is Tim Beckett, paediatrician at the hospital I'm interested in.'

She shook hands with Tim, noticing that although he was smiling more expansively than ever his brown eyes were alert. Tim put his pint of beer on their table and sat down.

'Always remember that I saw you first,' he said. 'I see you've got a drink. Could I ingratiate myself by fetching you a packet of crisps? Or even two packets? Angel, I would like to think that this is the start of a long and fruitful professional collaboration.'

She laughed. She'd never quite met anyone like this man.

'Among other things, Tim runs the hospital neonatal unit,' Mike explained. 'Like yours in Micklekirk but a bit larger.'

'It doesn't run, it staggers,' Tim said. 'If you say you're looking for a job now, Angel, I'll interview you in the next five minutes and you can start work tomorrow.'

'It can't be that bad!' With a slight shock she realised that Tim was only half joking.

'It is that bad. And it's a good department. We have a good medical staff, state-of-the-art equipment, a large training budget. We'll send you on any course that will benefit us. Say you'll join us tomorrow!'

All three were laughing now. 'If I come down I promise I'll work for you,' she said. 'But yours is a prestigious hospital. Why can't you get staff?'

'The young ones just can't afford to live round here,' he said bluntly. 'And we don't have any nurses' subsidised accommodation. Last week I had to pay five hundred pounds for a suitably qualified agency nurse to cover the weekend. She came down from Stafford.'

Angel winced. 'I can see you have problems.'

They spent the rest of the evening with Tim. He was an entertaining companion and they had lots to talk about. When he heard that they were going to visit his hospital the next day he pressed her to drop in at the neonatal unit.

'I'm off to the south coast early in the morning,' he said, 'but I could phone the sister in charge so she'll be expecting you.'

'I'd like to go then,' Angel said.

'I didn't set you up with Tim,' Mike said as the two of them walked back to the hotel. 'Our meeting there was pure chance.'

'I know that, Mike. And I'd like to look round his unit tomorrow.'

Mike left her in the unit next morning while he conferred with someone in senior management. 'I promise not to be longer than an hour,' he said. 'In fact what I have to say to this man should take ten minutes. The question is, will he listen?'

Sister Bell was about fifty-five, and had no thoughts of retiring. 'I started when I was sixteen and I have no intention of giving up when

I'm sixty. I need this job almost as much as it needs me.'

'Tim Beckett said you couldn't get staff because they couldn't afford to live around here.'

'He's right! I've been in my little house for thirty-one years now. It's not special but no incoming nurse could afford anything like it.'

Mike picked her up shortly after that and they wandered round the area. There were outdoor cafés—not much use at this time of year—bookshops, boutiques. She bought herself a dress for a surprisingly small amount. 'There are a lot of boutiques, they compete or go under,' Mike told her.

'Not exactly like Laxley. We've got a wool and haberdasher's there.'

Then, holding her new dress in its startlingly shiny purple carrier, she saw more of the area. There were a couple of parks, one of them with a fantastic view of the city of London. She could see many famous buildings, appearing like shadows in the grey mist.

In the evening they went into central London and saw a show, then had supper in a bistro afterwards.

On Sunday morning they met an estate agent who showed them round three different luxury flats. Angel quitc liked them all—until she saw the price of one. 'You could buy a farm for that in Laxley,' she squeaked. 'Quite a good farm, too.'

'I'm into hearts, not animals,' he told her.

Then they had lunch and made their way back to the airport.

'How did you like your trip?' he asked her, once they were airborne.

'You know very well that I had a fabulous time. I thought you were really good, Mike—you just showed me round and never once tried to sell me on the place. And I loved it. London's so exhilarating—it's like swallowing neat vodka.'

'I never knew you'd tried that,' he muttered. 'Don't forget, Angel, millions of people live quiet, ordinary lives in London. They do the shopping, they go to school, they see their friends. Just like in Laxley.'

'I know that, Mike. And I'm thinking.'

The weather in London had more or less been good—it had been warmer for a start and they'd had sunshine for most of the time. But when they got out of the plane it was raining. They set off in the car, and after half an hour Angel asked Mike to stop for a minute. He did and she stepped out. They were in the middle of the moors, only the odd distant light shining in the blackness. She stood, letting the rain touch her face, smelling the wetness. It was good to be back, she thought.

When she was back in the car she looked at Mike. He knew what she was feeling. But she remembered how he'd looked when he'd been talking about his work in the new wing of the hospital in London. This was his life's ambition come true. She couldn't ask him to change.

'You've got another three months here,' she said. 'At the end of that time, if we're still together and you ask me, I'll come down to London with you and Suzanne.'

He knew what it had cost her to say this. Gently he said, 'Just think about it, Angel. I'm not going to pressure you about it this time. We've got time to think, to consider. There's no reason why we should do what I want. You are a partner in this. And I still want above all to do what is best for Suzanne.'

That night, as she lay in his arms, she couldn't sleep. What should she do? She had loved her weekend in London. But she had loved coming home even more.

CHAPTER TEN

FOR the next two weekends Mike went back to London. There were things at the hospital he had to advise on, suggest, ask about. This suited Angel fine as she could take her turn in the Saturday and Sunday shifts and thus free herself for weekends later.

After the first trip he came back to tell her that one of the flats that they had viewed—in fact, the one she had liked the best—had gone. The agent had said that these days flats were at a premium, you had to jump while they were available. 'So I told him not to bother looking any more, I'd wait until I was in the job.'

'But I thought you were in a hurry?'

'I am in a hurry. But I thought if you were going to come with me, if there were to be three of us instead of just two—then I'd prefer a house to a flat. But I'm not pushing you, Angel. I said I would give you time.' He leaned over to kiss her. 'Never again will I pressure you.'

Her mother was discharged and came home. To Angel's amusement she seemed to have missed looking after Suzanne more than she had the company of her own daughter. She was still weak, of course, and Angel had to insist that Nancy still did most of the work. But their little family group was working well. She told Mike, 'Ma is really going to miss Suzanne when she goes.'

'I know,' he said sadly. He still came to see the baby every night, but he told Angel that he wouldn't stay the night while Marion was there. So every now and then she crept into his room in the residency. It was furtive and it was childish and she loved it. And she was getting to love Mike more and more.

'You're not the man I married,' she told him. 'You're more caring, you don't think you always know what is best.'

'Thank you for that compliment,' he said. 'Now it's my turn to be back-handed. You're more willing to listen to both sides of an argument. You can conceive that you might be wrong.'

'Only with great difficulty,' she told him.

They were so happy together. But she was aware that his time at Micklekirk was coming to an end. The hospital management committee had written to him asking him if he would like a full-time post as they would be pleased to offer him one. Typically, he showed the letter to Angel. 'This is a great hospital, Angel,' he said. 'The work here is hard but you've got a marvellous back-up and the management here is first rate.'

'But it's not introducing the work you want to do in London.'

'No. In a couple of years the techniques will be up here—but London will have to pioneer them. And I still want to do that.'

She would go to London with him if he asked her, she had promised him that. And she now knew that she wouldn't have been able to give up Suzanne. But as they gradually moved from winter into spring, she knew that it would be hard to tear herself away from this place.

They were invited to take Suzanne down to see Mark and Penny. Angel thought it was a lovely idea. Mike bought an expensive new baby seat for the car—he thought cheap ones were a false economy. 'I've heard of cheap ones breaking,' he told Angel. 'If it's safety you're worried about, you should get the best.'

Suzanne was a source of great interest to the twins, Sarah and Samantha. Judiciously, they compared her with their own little sister, Jennifer. 'You're not getting married, then?' Sarah asked. 'I thought you were supposed to be married if you had a baby.'

'She's not quite our baby,' Angel said, 'but we love her and we look after her.'

There was time to chat to Penny about the difficulties of bringing up a young child. 'I used to give out advice to young mums when I was a doctor,' Penny said. 'I feel quite guilty about it now. The facts were all correct, of course—but I got the feelings wrong. I never knew just how hard work babies were.'

'You can tell me,' Angel said feelingly, 'but at least we've got lots of help, and my Ma and Nancy are wonderful.'

Penny was sitting in a rocking chair, Jennifer on her lap. 'I don't care what the experts say,' she said, rocking a little faster, 'I think every baby needs a father. Certainly every mother needs a husband—or partner, if you like. Work is so much easier if it can be shared.'

'If the partner knows what he's doing,' Angel pointed out. 'In fact, many of my mums don't have much idea. They bring their own mothers sometimes, and that way we get some sense out of them.'

'Which brings us,' Penny said slowly, 'to young Suzanne there having both a mother and a father. Poor little mite didn't do very well the first time round, did she?' Mark and Penny had been told the circumstances of Suzanne's birth.

'We—well, Mike and me together—are doing the best we can,' Angel said, 'though there are problems.'

'Hmm. Mark tells me that Mike has this offer of a wonder job in London. Tell me if you don't want to talk about it, but it's obvious from seeing you and Mike together that you're...you're...'

'Yes we are,' Angel said. 'I love him and I'd marry him again tomorrow but... D'you mind if I tell you all about it?'

It was surprisingly helpful, talking to a third person. Penny wasn't involved and she could see both points of view with equal clarity.

'You've got a problem,' she said. 'I'm not going to offer any advice, because I can't think of anything to say. Just one thing. I don't think any marriage is off to a good start if one partner sacrifices everything to please the other. There's always some room for negotiation if you can find it.'

'I hope so,' said Angel.

They had intended to stay till late evening, but the weather forecast was bad and Mark and Penny encouraged them to make an early start. 'You have to cross the Pennines,' Mark pointed out, 'and that can be tricky. Don't worry, we'll be over to see you soon enough.'

In fact, the journey over the M62 was easy. Mike had a four-wheel-drive car. Angel felt very safe in the warmth, and the lashing wind and bitter rain hardly affected them at all. They made good time, dropped down towards flatter country and turned left onto the A1M. Then they had to turn left again. This was still a main road, but more lonely, crossing through wilder country. And then a warning cut in on the radio. There had been a crash ahead. Long delays were anticipated. Mike pulled in. 'Let's have a look at the map,' he said.

This was her home country, they were only about thirty miles from Micklekirk. 'We can turn off here,' she said pointing. 'It's only a small road but it'll get us there. And in winter there'll hardly be a vehicle on it. It's mostly a summer road for walkers.'

'That sounds fine. We'll be home in time for an early supper.'

Five minutes later they did turn off. The road was narrow, with frequent bends, and he had to slow down. There was nothing to see but blackness ahead, cut only by their headlights. And the rain drummed down on them. Nothing passed. The only sign of life was an occasional roadside farm building and all were without lights.

Angel wound down her window a little and sniffed the night air. 'I love it up here when it blows,' she said. 'There's nowhere else like it. In London when there's a wind all you get is cars crashing and slates falling off roofs. But here you feel as if you're one with nature.'

His voice was amused. 'Are you trying to tell me something?'

'No! Not at all. What I said, it just slipped out. I said we would decide later and I meant it.'

She could tell he wasn't angry. 'It sounded as if you were saying that you couldn't be happy in London.'

'No. Well, perhaps... Mike, what is most important is that I want to be with you. Wherever you are, that's where I'll be happiest. I want to spend my life with you...if you want me.'

He reached over to stroke her hair. 'Oh, I want you all right. Life without you would be insupportable. I can't imagine...'

He wasn't driving fast. They were skirting the top of a small valley. In it was a stream, now swollen by the rain. Gently, they turned a corner. The car slowed and lurched to the left. Angel thought they had skidded. Then she screamed as they rolled over sideways. For a moment she knew they were upside down, her body flopped forward against the restraining seat belt. She heard a curse from Mike, a wail from the terrified baby. Then there was a crash, the sound of rending metal and an agonising pain in her shoulder. Then she lost consciousness.

She was lying on her side. She was cold, she was wet, and when she tried to sit up the pain in her shoulder was so great that she screamed again.

'Angel, Angel, don't lose it now! Angel, you've got to stay awake. Just lie there, feel your body a bit at a time, tell me where you're injured.' Mike's voice was desperate, coming from somewhere above her. Then there was another noise—the cry of a baby. How was Suzanne?

Injured and frightened though she was, her professional training came through. That wasn't the sound of an injured baby. For the moment, Suzanne was all right.

'Just give me a minute, Mike,' she muttered. 'I don't think I'm too badly hurt. Yes, I am! My clavicle is broken!' When she ran her hand over the shoulder bone she could easily feel the fracture. 'What happened?'

'I don't know. We came off the road, but I just don't know why. Now, if I can wriggle round… There should be a torch in this side pocket—got it!'

A moment later the torch flicked on, and by its dim light she could see the plight they were in. The car was on its side in the stream. Water was pouring through the broken windscreen and across her body. Dangling precariously above her was Mike, held fast by his seat belt, his body twisted in what must have been an agonising position. And behind her was Suzanne, still in her safety seat. But the seat was wet through. The tiny girl must be soaking.

'I had my mobile on the dashboard,' Mike said. 'It must have fallen—can you feel around see if you can find it?'

The pain and the cold were as strong as ever, but she was slowly growing more conscious of things. Mike's voice was clear enough, but there was a roughness to it that made her realise he was in pain.

'Are you injured, Mike? Are you all right?'

This time she heard his gasp of pain. 'I have been better. My leg is smashed—in at least two places, I think. One thing is certain—I can't walk. Now, can you find the mobile?'

She felt round about, underneath herself, being careful not to cut herself on jagged bits of metal or glass. A small, oblong piece of something—the mobile! She lifted it into the thin light of the torch. 'Broken,' she said, 'completely, utterly broken. With a mobile we could have sent for help. We could have—'

'Angel!' Mike's voice echoed through the car. 'We are trained medical staff and we have the life of a child in our hands. Now, we don't panic and we don't give way to shock. You can fight it! Wriggle into the back of the car, next to Suzanne. Then I'll drop down next to you.'

His words about Suzanne had made her determined. She pulled herself half-upright, managed to use her legs to push herself into the back of the car. If she held her shoulders back the agony was… Well, it was endurable—just. She was still half in the water, just below Suzanne. Almost automatically she reached for the wailing infant, stroked her cheek and muttered, 'There, darling, there. Soon have you dry and warm and comfy again.'

Mike managed to undo his seat belt and somehow broke his fall as he dropped to where she had been. 'On the back shelf behind you, Angel. There's a first-aid box—can you pass it to me?'

She screamed again when she had to twist. There was crepitus—the two ends of her broken clavicle grinding against each other. But she found the box and she passed it to him. 'Now, turn your back to me,' he said.

She felt him knotting bandages round both shoulders and then pulling them tight across her back. It hurt a bit, but she knew that for a while it would stop the bone ends rubbing together. 'And here's a plaster for your forehead.' She hadn't known she'd been cut. What was one more drip among all the others?

'Why has Suzanne stopped crying?' His voice was anxious again. Angel felt for her little charge, put her head close to the baby's head.

'She's getting chilled,' she said. 'All her bedding is wet through and there isn't anything dry on her. Mike, she'll get hypothermia!'

'I know that! Can you get her out, strip her and pass her to me?'

'That'll make things even worse!'

Now there was a tremble to his voice, the tremble of pain. 'She is cold and wet, I am warm and dry. I'll warm her for a minute. Now get her!'

Angel's fingers were now beginning to numb, the cold affecting her more and more.

But she managed to fumble the straps undone, pull away the damp clothing and pass the wet little body to Mike. He undid his anorak, pulled up his sweater and crammed Suzanne next to his skin. 'I can spare the warmth,' he said. 'She's chilly but there isn't much of her.' Only his laboured breathing told her what he was suffering.

'Now, Angel, this is up to you. I can't walk and no one else is going to come down this road tonight. We have to look after ourselves—and Suzanne. You'll have to get out of the car, then you'll have to walk back down the road. You can carry Suzanne. We passed an old climbing hut about three miles back. Break a window and climb in. There should be blankets there, perhaps something to eat. You and Suzanne get dry, get warm and then wait.'

'What about you?'

'I'll be all right. Don't, whatever you do, leave her. You've both got to get warm and dry. I'm big and strong, I'll survive.'

'But I can't leave you here. You might…you might…'

'Angel, listen to me, my love. You're going to need all your strength. Now, pass me that baby seat—just thc bare plastic—throw all the wet stuff out. Then get out of the car.'

She was past arguing now. She did as he'd told her, somehow pushing open the door that was above her, managing to climb out into the rain, sitting on the side of the car and then sliding off. It was agonising.

'Now, reach through the front windscreen and take Suzanne.' She paddled through the stream and leaned down to do as he'd said, peering at the little bundle he pushed out to her. 'Mike! You've wrapped all your clothes round her! You'll freeze to death!'

The baby was wrapped in his shirt and sweater and round the seat he had placed his anorak.

'I won't freeze to death as quickly as she could. I'm fit and strong, I can do sufficient exercise to keep the blood circulating. Now, stop talking and move! Here, take the torch.'

'I can't leave you to—'

'You can and you will. And Angel…I love you!'

Was his voice weaker now? He had said he loved her. She wondered if…if he was giving her something to remember him by. With a sob she stooped to pick up the baby seat. 'I love you, too, Mike. And I'm leaving you.' Then she started to scramble upwards.

As she did so Angel saw what had happened to them. The road was undercut, the earth underneath it had just dropped away. Then the tarmac had broken when the weight of the car had driven over it.

She couldn't climb straight upwards, she had to follow a diagonal course, aiming for where the slope was easiest. A couple of times she fell, but she kept going and she held onto the baby seat.

She could only bear to hold the seat in her right hand. Her left hand, the side of the fractured clavicle, she tucked into the top pocket of her anorak. This eased the pain just a little.

In time she made the top of the slope and climbed onto the road. The wind was blowing stronger up here, chilling her even more. Perhaps the exercise would warm her up. She remembered having passed the climbing hut. She could make it. She had to make it.

Walking was agonising, and the wind was against her. She clutched the seat to her and walked on. The bandage across her shoulders made holding the seat harder—but Suzanne didn't weigh very much. She could do it. She had to.

For how long she walked she didn't know. Then suddenly she found herself slipping, tripping over into the heather. Perhaps she should sit and rest for a while. She was exhausted. She tried to dry a hand and slipped it inside the seat. Suzanne was still warm. That was good.

So she crouched by the side of the road for a minute. Only when she started to feel warm and sleepy did she know she had to move. If she could feel pain then she was still alive. She managed to stand, managed to walk on. She was cold, she was wet but she had to keep moving. Mike and Suzanne needed her.

After a while she knew she had to stop to rest again. But this time she wouldn't sit down. She'd just turn her back to the storm and wait a couple of minutes. If she sat down she knew she might not stand again.

She walked, one foot in front of the other, just one foot at a time, then another. Don't think about how far there was to go. Just one foot in front of the other, that was all. And she had to keep her eyes open! The rain and the wind lashed them, but if she tried to shut her eyes she staggered off the road.

And she was so cold.

Finally she could go no further. She had to sit down for a minute, she had to rest her eyes, her weary legs, do something to ease the chill that invaded her whole body…

'What are you doing out on a night like this?'

What? That was a stupid question. Everyone knew she was… What was she doing out on a night like this? No, it was an interesting question. And suddenly she was bathed in light.

She managed to open her eyes again. There were men, tough-looking men in bad-weather gear, men who knew what they were doing. She saw a four-wheel-drive vehicle, its lights shining on her.

'Get out of the way and let me take a look at her.' Interesting. That was a female voice. So they weren't all men. The female seemed to put an arm round her and said, 'What're you carrying that's so—? My God, there's a baby here!'

She had very little strength left, but she knew she had to say something before she went to sleep. 'Two miles up the road there's a car in the river. There's a man inside it and he's…he's… Please, keep the baby warm, her name's Suzanne and—'

'We'll see to everything now,' a voice said comfortingly. 'Let's get your baby inside where it's warm and you climb in here.' An arm came round her shoulders, the broken bone rubbed and she screamed again. Then there was only comforting darkness.

It was like a weird dream. Angel wasn't sure what was happening, she only knew that she didn't have to worry any more. Other people would worry and she could rest. There were people around her, the sound of car engines and wonderful, wonderful warmth. Later on there was a tiny chill as her clothes were pulled off and people were doing things to her. But soon she was warm again. Then more comforting darkness.

* * *

She felt as if she had been beaten with a mallet. She was weaker than she had ever been in her life before, all she wanted to do was rest. But there was something she had to do. With an effort she opened her eyes, gazed at the white ceiling. What was she doing here?

'So you're awake at last.'

A cheerful voice. She turned her head to see a nurse. Angel thought she vaguely recognised her, she'd seen her somewhere... Recollection came flooding back!

'Suzanne! Where's Suzanne?'

The nurse heard the terror in her voice. 'Suzanne is fine,' she said. 'She's down in the baby unit, as happy as anything and no worse for her experience. Your mother is fussing round her. They're keeping her in just to make sure—but she should be discharged this afternoon.'

'And Mike? Is he all right?'

This nurse seemed to know everything. 'Mr Gilmour is two floors down in the orthopaedic ward. He's got plaster up to his thigh and a bandage on his head, but he seems to have survived well enough. When you've had some breakfast and the doctor has had a look at you, perhaps he'll let us put you in a wheelchair and you can go down to see him.'

'So I'm in…'

'You're in your own hospital, Micklekirk. Brought into A and E earlyish last night. You were lucky. A party of walkers found you as they were driving to a climbing hut. They got to you just in time.' For the first time the nurse's face was serious. 'They say you couldn't have walked much further. And if you'd stopped…'

If she'd stopped? Angel thought about it, and burst into tears.

The doctor came to look at her and then her mother called in to see her. She said that Suzanne was fine and that she would take her home later. Nancy would help, as always. Marion was serene, confident that now all would be well. Angel was glad of that, she didn't want any more emotion.

Slowly, the feeling of weakness and the weepiness disappeared. 'You've given your body a bit of a battering,' the doctor said. 'Now it's getting its own back. But you'll feel a bit better later on today.'

As a nurse, she was curious. 'Just what is wrong with me?'

'When you were brought in you were in shock,' the doctor said. 'How you kept going along that road I just don't know. But you did. Sometimes, when you've just got to do something, the body finds that it can do it. Anyway, you're paying it back now. You had a nasty bang on your head, but you weren't seriously concussed. You were suffering from hypothermia, but one of those climbers was a paramedic. He knew just how to keep your condition from getting worse until we got our hands on you.'

'And my shoulder?'

'Fractured clavicle. Did you know that of all the bones in the body, the clavicle is fastest to heal? Interesting, isn't it? No one quite knows why. And of all the bones on the body it is probably the easiest to knit, even though it's almost impossible to control movement.'

'Fascinating,' Angel muttered. In fact, it was fascinating, but she found the doctor's enthusiasm just a bit hard to bear. She was the one suffering the pain. 'So how will you set it?'

'We won't. We took X-rays last night—there was some overlapping and shortening but there was no need for any great effort at reduction. What we've done is just an elaboration of those bandages you had on when you came in. You can feel there's a stockinette pad over each shoulder? Well they're tied together across your back and pulled tight to keep your shoulders back. That's all we need. Oh, and you'd better keep the injured arm in a sling for a day or two.'

When she learned that she wasn't seriously injured she felt better. 'Have you seen the man who was brought in with me?' she asked, 'Mr Gilmour?'

'I've seen him but he's not my patient. His leg is in a worse state than your shoulder, but ultimately there's absolutely no reason why he shouldn't make a complete recovery.' The doctor grinned. 'He refused to be anaesthetised until he'd heard that you and the little girl were all right.'

She felt much better after a light lunch. Her lethargy wasn't so pronounced and the nurse decided she could be taken to visit Mike. 'I'll just phone to see if he's fit to receive visitors,' she said.

So Angel was wheeled along the corridor and down in the lift. She didn't like it very much. This was her hospital, usually she walked along fast and proud like the other nurses. She'd rather be a nurse than a patient.

Mike was in a side ward, a little room to himself. The nurse wheeled Angel beside the bed, so that Angel could hold his hand, perhaps even lean over and kiss him.

'I'll leave you, I'm going to pinch a cup of tea,' the nurse said. 'Back in a quarter of an hour and don't over-excite yourselves!'

'I'd like the chance,' muttered Mike.

'You look like I feel,' Angel said candidly. She hadn't realised before, but he had injured his head, too. There was a patch where the hair had been shaved, and a dressing covered it. His leg had been plastered, she could see the outline under the sheet. And his face looked—well, battered. Not physically but emotionally. 'How do you feel, anyway?'

He considered. 'My leg itches and my head aches but I'm warm, reasonably comfortable and I know I'll survive. Compared to how I was last night, I'd say I was in pretty good shape. How're you, Angel? I know Suzanne's OK.'

'Fractured clavicle and a head injury like you. Also like you, I know I'll survive.' Then she burst into tears yet again. 'Mike, why are we talking to each other like this? I love you and you nearly died!'

He reached for her hand, squeezed it. 'It's only emotion, sweetheart. Too much to face up to. You can't help thinking about what might have happened. But it didn't happen. We're all right.'

She found a tissue, wiped her eyes. 'Yes we're all right. And it makes all our other troubles seem trivial! Whatever happens, we've got each other.'

'And Suzanne,' he said.

'Yes, and Suzanne. My mother said she was gurgling with pleasure when they put her into her cot last night.'

'Something to tell her children in years to come.' He had twisted his head to look at her, now he let it drop back to the pillow and stared at the ceiling. 'I've been doing some thinking this morning, Angel. The orthopaedics man has been in to see me. He said I wasn't fit to make any kind of decisions yet but that after a couple of days I can have my secretary in to take letters.'

'You and decisions,' she said.

'Last night I forced you out into the rain with a baby. I did it because I thought that was the best chance for you and Suzanne to survive. And when you'd gone I lay there, listening to the rain and wondering if I'd sent you out to die. We could have clung together, there was some body warmth between us.'

'Not enough. Suzanne would probably have died. You forced me out but I needed it. You made the right decision, Mike. Be pleased about that.'

'I heard that at the most you could only have kept going for another ten minutes.'

'Ten minutes was long enough,' she muttered.

'Just. Now, I'll tell you what I've been thinking. When I get my secretary here, when I'm allowed to make decisions, I'll write to the London hospital and say that there is no way that I'll be able to take up the post in the foreseeable future. They must find someone else. If necessary, I can recommend someone.'

'But, Mike! You've been working towards this job for years!'

'And I'm turning it down. It's a question of priorities, Angel. I want to be with you and I want to be with Suzanne and I want to stay here.'

'You're just saying that to please me!'

'Can you think of a better reason to do something? Don't worry about my professional future. Micklekirk is an excellent regional hospital. I want to stay and work here. In a couple of years I'll be able to introduce the techniques I studied in America.'

It was too much to take in. This was the best news she ever could have imagined—she couldn't have written a better scenario herself. But did she believe Mike? Was he still affected by the accident, still weak? She couldn't take advantage of him if he wasn't sure of what he was saying.

'We'll forget you said that,' she said. 'In another week or two, when you're a lot better, you can tell me again. You know it's what I want to hear, but I want you to have time to think, to decide. I love you Mike. I can wait for you.'

'If I had lost you, out there is the wilderness, I would have wanted to die, too. I won't allow myself to risk losing you again, so I've made my decision,' he said. 'I love you Angel. Suzanne and I belong here, with you. I'm asking you now...will you marry me?'

Looking into the clear depths of his eyes, Angel knew for sure. Mike had meant every word he had said, and he heart lifted.

'You're asking me to become your wife and Suzanne's mother,' she murmured softly, with a smile. 'How could I ever refuse, my love?'

MEDICAL ROMANCE™

Titles for the next six months…

August

GUILTY SECRET	Josie Metcalfe
PARTNERS BY CONTRACT	Kim Lawrence
MORGAN'S SON	Jennifer Taylor
A VERY TENDER PRACTICE	Laura MacDonald

September

INNOCENT SECRET	Josie Metcalfe
HER DR WRIGHT	Meredith Webber
THE SURGEON'S LOVE-CHILD	Lilian Darcy
BACK IN HER BED	Carol Wood

October

A WOMAN WORTH WAITING FOR	Meredith Webber
A NURSE'S COURAGE	Jessica Matthews
THE GREEK SURGEON	Margaret Barker
DOCTOR IN NEED	Margaret O'Neill

0702 LP 2P P1 Medica

0702 LP 2P P2 Medical